Rosemary Anne Mills is a female writer who considers herself to be a 'storyteller'. A writer who is well-read and enjoys mixing reality with Speculative, Science Fiction. She aims to encourage the reader to question the main character's journey of self-doubt and consider the importance of 'free will'. Her stories are written for the reader to ask the question, 'What if?'

I dedicate this novel to all those people who enjoy reading humorous social history, combined with Science Fiction and believe in Angels.

To my brothers: John and Robert James Mills, for without their loving encouragement and faith in me – this story may never have been sent to my publisher.

Rosemary Anne Mills

THE QUESTFUL SEEKER

AUSTIN MACAULEY PUBLISHERS™

LONDON • CAMBRIDGE • NEW YORK • SHARJAH

Austin Macauley is committed to publishing works of quality and integrity. In this spirit, we are proud to offer this book to our readers; however, the story, the experiences, and the words are the author's alone.

A CIP catalogue record for this title is available from the British Library.

ISBN 9781528914970 (Paperback)
ISBN 9781528914987 (Hardback)
ISBN 9781528961066 (ePub e-book)

www.austinmacauley.com

First Published (2020)
Austin Macauley Publishers Ltd
25 Canada Square
Canary Wharf
London
E14 5LQ

The Arrival

The sun rose in the East, early that May spring morning 1953, and as such the air temperature climbed at a rapid pace, while the wild birds left their overnight shelters of the surrounding hedgerows and began their early morning chorus with unified melodious sounds. Blackbirds, Thrushes and Robins completely dominated the smaller birds' delicate, shorter, musical shrills, as they too announced their presence.

Air was fresh, as the glistening, liquid dew vapour rose from the cold ground and left a lowly scent upon the surrounding flora and fauna. Wild pink rhododendron with their large clusters of showy, trumpet-shaped flowers, bright, sweet-scented, yellow and pink Honeysuckle flowers, and soft, pale pink blooms of the wild dog rose, with its delicate scent, added to nature's perfume, intermingled over the surrounding fields and hedgerows.

It would have been the perfect epitome of the English countryside, if it had not been for the dominant intrusive presence of a railway station, which sat high on a plateau, interrupting the natural beauty of the scenery.

Nevertheless, this natural landscape encircled the outer boundaries of the station and enriched one's senses as the flora and fauna's fragrance filled the air and that railway station came back to life.

The time was close to 8am and the station was already busy with people who waited for their early train, which allowed them to commute to their workplaces outside the village. Railway staff busied themselves and prepared for the first early morning train that was due to arrive any moment.

The railway employees greeted all their customers who had already entered the station.

A latecomer was seen running up the cobbled stone lane towards the entrance gate to Platform One, and many waiting passengers turned their heads and watched in amusement as a middle-aged, bald, overweight man who had tried his best to run up the cobblestoned lane. He carried a small black leather briefcase in one hand and a black, felt bowler hat in the other and although he tried to run, his huffing and puffing was heard on both platforms. By the time he reached the old, turn-style, iron entrance gate, his face was flushed, and pearls of sweat covered his face. When he tilted his face upwards, it glowed even redder with embarrassment, as he heard an elderly porter shout out to his work companion,

"Hey, look at this bloke, running as if his life depended upon him catching the 8am train."

The porter then laughed and shouted to the man,

"Early to bed, early to rise, young man."

The late passenger was too puffed to answer the porter but lifted his left hand up in the air, in the form of a V-sign. The porters shook their heads in dismay and turned away from the man in disgust. Then the head porter noticed that latecomer had walked across the walkway to access Platform 2, on the opposite side, and rudely bellowed out to the junior porters,

"Young people today, they have not got any bloody manners."

That latecomer arrived hot and bothered because he had overdressed that morning, in a winter weight, navy, pinstriped three-piece suit. A white shirt, black tie and black socks inside highly polished black leather, lace-up shoes, which allowed him no respite from the powerful rays of the sun.

The man's embarrassment had not yet ended, for when he reached Platform 2, he realised everyone else who travelled to Cheshire's main station were situated on Platform 1. He dropped his head in despair and speedily joined the waiting passengers on Platform 1.

Fellow passengers were amused, but as no-one wanted to upset the latecomer, only a few raised eyebrows caught the eye of the confused traveller. He proceeded to wipe the sweat from his brow with his neatly ironed, white cotton handkerchief. He had chosen to stand next to two elderly women, because they were dressed neatly in matching navy and white striped, cotton summer frocks, with hems which stopped just above their knees.

Indeed, he felt comfortable in their presence, especially as they were wearing wedding rings and obviously retired. He had not felt obliged to make idle conversation, because they chatted quite happily together.

As he moved a little closer, he noted a light, fresh scent of starch, and when the women walked around, the smell of 'Lilly of the Valley' drifted towards him. He breathed-in their cologne and sighed; for his wife also favoured the same scent; this connection to his own wife allowed him to relax, despite having been close to two stranglers.

Seemingly, he thought, 'their summer dresses were chosen to tone with their matching navy, summer peep-toe leather sandals and white bolero jackets.'

They were heavily busted women, whose dress-sense he thought, 'epitomised summer outfits worn, by ladies of a 'certain age'; and the plump man admired how elegant they looked. His daydreaming ended abruptly when the station clock struck eight times.

The heavily built, middle-aged man's breathing became heavier and heavier, due to the sun's intense rays, but he was not on his own, for and the two senior friends gently, patted the perspiration from their faces; with their light cotton floral handkerchiefs.

His admiration of the women, quickly turned to disapproval, when he caught a reek of, 'Face powder, oh no! How distasteful,' he mumbled under his breath, and he turned his head away, in-case they had heard his grumbles,

'Two middle-aged women should not wear black cake mascara on their eyelashes and bright pink blusher high on their cheekbones. For goodness sake, such heavy make-up, makes them look like Tarts.'

The overheavy man forgot himself and tutted, before saying "I am just an old-fashioned sort of man, who prefers the clean, fresh look of a countrywoman; who only wear a modest amount of lipstick at best!"

His trivial rudeness, was noted by the two friends, but Gladys eye-balled him, before saying,

"Miserable old Sod! I pity your wife."

Her friend giggled, but decided it best to re-direct her friend,

"Goodness me, Nelly, are we going to have a heat wave today?"

Glady replied, "I was listening to the weather forecast on the radio just before I set out this morning and the weatherman stated that it's expected to get into the 80s today."

"Cor blimey! If it gets that hot, we are going to melt away, Gladys," she replied.

Both women placed their wicker shopping baskets on the ground beside them, then proceeded to remove their summer jackets, folded them neatly before they placed them into their baskets. That rotund man stood beside the two women transfixed, as he thought, 'My goodness, they seem to mirror-image each other's movements.'

Indeed, their unified movements amused him so much so, that he could not remove the smirk that was set upon his face.

Meanwhile, several pretty, young girls, stood close by, but at a discreet distance from the older women. The girls giggled and swopped details of their latest boyfriend conquests, much to the disgust of the two older women, who listened in on their conversation.

The group of young women stood waiting for their early morning train to the nearest town, where the girls worked in various dress shops. Whereas the older women had planned a day out, which had included shopping in the local indoor market, before enjoying a meal out together.

Suddenly, the head porter announced the 8am train was on time, and sternly reminded them all,

"Don't get too close to the edge of that platform! We don't want any accidents now, do we?"

When the porter turned his head, he noticed a small, green Ford van, which had been driven up the cobbled lane and parked close to the entrance's turn-style gate.

A tall, dark-haired, slim young man was dressed-in a white cotton T-shirt over faded, blue denim jeans; as he emerged from the van. The teenager had large bare feet, which slithered about in his over-sized, leather Jesus sandals. The youth stepped out of his van, turned around, leaned over his driving seat, and pulled out several large bundles of newspapers. Each package was tied neatly together with string, and after he emerged from his vehicle, he shouted, "Anyone want a copy of today's papers?"

Shortly afterwards, a coal wagon arrived at the station, proceeded towards the shunting yard, and delivered that day's load of coal.

More people started to arrive on foot and rushed towards the station's turn-style gate,

'Hurry along now!" shouted out the porter.

Soon, the whole railway station buzzed with noise. The porter moved towards the entrance gate and opened it for the newsagent and the Newsagent walked onto the station platform, where he proceeded to sell his various newspapers to the waiting passengers.

A momentary atmosphere of excitement and activity resulted when passengers exchanged their coins for their chosen periodical. and the porter complained, 'What a hullabaloo'.

A conversation took place between two waiting passengers. One smartly dressed businessman turned to his colleague who stood next to him and asked, "Do you think we are all about to enter into a nuclear war, Jameson?"

Jameson replied, "It does not look too good at present! With this 'Cold War' re-emerging and constant skirmishes escalating between the United States of America and its adversaries. Does it? We have to stay positive, despite the forthcoming feeling of impending doom hovering over us all once more!"

Paradoxically, at the same time, a vortex appeared on the horizon where a portal connected two different dimensions. A ghostly old Victorian steam engine emerged, which pulled several passenger carriages, a little worse for wear and out of time and place.

The steam train and its carriages glided downwards towards Haven's Railway Station, surrounded by dense smoke from its steam engine.

No one reacted to that strange and frightening phenomenon, which appeared from a heavenly gateway.

The intense, natural sunlight blinded people's view of that strange, incoming train, which had entered the station adjacent to Platform 1.

The train glided through an invisible curtain, as 'silent as the grave', having not touched the ground, but all was about to change.

Suddenly, the old train jerked, wavered in motion; as its engine brakes screamed loudly, which should have pierced a person's eardrums. Smoke continued to billow from its chimney, over the station and waiting passengers. As the engine's rusty, old iron wheels clanged noisily, they aligned themselves onto the single line railway track of Platform 1.

The air was filled with the stench of Sulphur fumes, just as one of the old women, standing on Platform 1, said to her friend, "Poo! Gladys, what a stink. Can you smell it? Its' near choking me. Did you see that?"

Her friend replied, "I cannot smell anything, Nelly. Are you sure? All those cigarettes you smoked over the years, has dulled your senses and, making you feel ill? Surely, it is time you gave them up, isn't it!"

Nelly gave her friend such a dirty look, Gladys shrugged her shoulders and said, "Have it your own way! The inside of your lungs must be near-ruined, from all that tobacco smoke you have inhaled. Being a chain-smoker will only add nails to your coffin, my dear!"

Nelly did not hear her friend's advice, because her eyes were transfixed upon that incoming, old steam train, especially its carriages; which appeared to be void of passengers. She could not believe her eyes, as it had been years since steam engines had entered Haven's railway station.

"Not since the lines went electric," she cried out.

"What the hell are you talking about, Nelly? asked Gladys.

"Why, can you not see it?" cried out Nelly in despair.

"See what?" said Gladys.

Nelly blinked then rubbed her eyes, not once but twice and finally realised that there was no steam train there after all. Feeling foolish she grumbled, "Must layoff the stout at supper time."

Her friend, Gladys, started to laugh out loud.

"I could have sworn that just for a moment, I saw a steam train coming towards us, but there is nothing there now. It must have been an illusion; due to my indigestion, playing me up again. Perhaps, caused by that extra cheese 'n' onion sandwich, I ate with a glass of stout at supper last night."

Gladys looked at her friend, threw her head back and laughed and said,

"More like you are tired, Nelly. Bet you and that old husband of yours were 'at it' half the night, and most likely you were too sozzled to remember anything. Drinking too much stout late at night is just not good for your health, girl. Mark my words, old or not, men take advantage of us women when we are intoxicated, as men do!"

"Don't talk soft, Gladys; I don't remember any 'hanky-panky' going on!"

"Exactly my point, Nelly, we never do at our age."

"Let's admit it, at our age, it takes our men so long to get going, we just 'lie back and think of England' – as the old saying goes."

They both giggled at the thought.

The old ladies looked at each other giggled, like teenage girls, and laughed until tears ran down their cheeks.

"Get away with you," said Nelly, and afterwards she shook her head and laughed again, before she explained, "my Jack is near 70 now, and finding 'it', would be an achievement at his age. Blimey! I should be so lucky."

At which point, they again both broke out into hysterical laughter, before Nelly said, "Funny thing though, that old steam engine looked real to me, especially as I could see the smoke – even smell the dirty, stuff. Maybe you are right – I should cut down on my late suppers and try and drink less stout."

Both women nodded their heads in agreement.

However, that ghostly old train had appeared from nowhere, with its carriages on tow. It finally came to a screaming halt when its iron-wheels were located firmly down on the electrified railway track.

Noticeably, the first carriage stood out from the rest, because it had been painted in a distinctive forest green, with a faint red stripe around its window frames.

Haven's railway station was busy with the activity of people, especially the porters who busied themselves, when they moved the day's 'out-going' mailbags, from the station master's office onto platform 1. The porters placed that day's mail into a large, heavy, iron-wheeled trolley, which had a handle at one end and a cage at the other. When the mail was all placed in the metal cage, the porters manually pulled the mail trolly across the platform, and shouted out,

"Watch yourselves, ladies. We don't want to damage those pretty legs of yours."

The porters, like the waiting passengers, were oblivious to the presence of the old steam engine and its carriages – it may as well not have been there!

A waiting passenger asked the head porter, "Is the train running on time?" The porter checked the time on his Fob watch, then he tapped its glass face methodically, before he replaced it within his top lapel pocket, and made sure its chain was secure within his buttonhole.

The porter then announced,

"The *8am* train due in on Platform 1 is running on schedule."

Still, no one took any notice of that unscheduled old train, which stood next to Platform 1, or the fact that one carriage stood out from the rest.

Sequestered inside that mysterious carriage was a blurry shadow of a man who was wearing a soldier's uniform; slightly worse for wear.

Time Stands Still

Fundamentally, time itself was a paradox for the soldier, who had been suddenly thrust into a situation that his mind could not have grasped. Although he knew quite well that his journey had been extended; the details seemed quite obscure. His mind was unable to comprehend the reality of his present situation.

He took a deep breath to steady his nerves, in hope it would help him to focus his mind, because he still had no recollection of how he had journeyed to this point in time.

That soldier's anxious state of mind had given him an intense feeling of loneliness, which overwhelmed him, as he cried out,

"Why are there no other passengers in this carriage? How long have I been asleep?"

The soldier pondered on the possible answers to his questions, he allowed his eyes to wander around the carriage, which left the soldier bewildered,

"It has been such a long time since I remember being in a railway carriage like this one, perhaps, when I left home to join the army. I remember. I remember!" he cried out.

The soldier tried his best to recall memories, which would have given him answers and may have explained his present predicament. But his mind was blank, and it pained him to think aloud, let alone recall details from his past.

Suddenly, perseverance paid off,

"I remember while waiting for our train, in a London railway station, there was a man who had taken photographs of us all, then demanded money. What a bloody con-artist! We had no choice but to pay the thief, and I ended up paying for my mate's photograph too, as he was broke. But I cannot remember the name of the ship, which took us all to Egypt – strange that!" he moaned.

An image of his disgruntled face came into his mind, which did not enlighten his sombre mood at all.

He continued to express his anger out loud, "Bloody hell, I was so mad at that photographer, but it was a case of paying up, or he would have reported us to the police, and the army would not have been too pleased. Any trouble with the law may have resulted in us all in jail. So, I had no choice, but to pay the crook as he had us 'over the coals' and he knew it. Bloody con-artist, he knew we could not afford to miss our train connection to Dover; where we were due to board the ship that was to take our unit to Egypt."

As he sighed his shoulders drooped with despair, which resulted in his mind going blank. His melancholy overpowered him to such an extent, he felt quite unsteady on his feet, so he placed his hands upon the back of the red leather seat and leaned forward and supported his weary body. He hoped he would be able to make sense of his present circumstances.

The soldier told himself,

"Need to get a grip, mate; you'll be alright once your strength returns."

As the soldier looked around, he perceived the interior of that ghostly railway carriage, as a mirror-image of similar carriages shown in films, he had seen at the cinema, with his friends, "Blimey. Its' been a long time since I was able to watch any film, let alone visit a cinema. It looks to me as if someone has played a sick joke on me."

The soldier's senses were on overload and when he instinctively sniffed the air, he almost choked.

"Yes, yes, tobacco," he laughed.

He continued, "Bloody hell, with a stink like this, there must have been a fair few ciggies and pipes smoked in here over the past years. The smell of tobacco is embedded in these seats. They stink to high Heaven!"

Although that carriage was distinctively grubby, it was a visual display of vintage glamour, with its quality materials, manufactured to withstand the test of time.

Indeed, the interior of that ghostly railway carriage was a mirror image of railway carriages portrayed in old 20c. films, a specific time-set, an epitome of middle-class luxury.

He sensed the overall care which must have gone into its design, despite its grubbiness. He admired the brocade curtains that were decorated with large heavily embroidered flowers in rich toning red silks and cream full-length linen linings; clipped into oversized wooden rings. In turn, the curtain rings were attached to wooden pine curtain poles that extended the length of the sash windows on both sides of the carriage; held firmly in place with matching tiebacks.

Identical high-backed, buttoned, red leather seats faced each other within that carriage and extended to three-quarters of the height of the wagon. Trimmed at the top with stained pine, placed lengthwise in a tongue and groove manner. Each seat had been designed to seat at least six passengers on each side, and bamboo-framed luggage racks hung over each bench with stretch netting attached; which enabled passengers to place their precious possessions in a safe place. The shelves were fixed to the walls by five strategically placed decorative black, cast iron supports that were both decorative and practicable and discouraged excess luggage cluttering up the floor and seating spaces.

"All this space and only me in here," the soldier cried out, as his attention turned to the floor areas. "The floor and ceiling are both made from dark stained, heavy pine planking, which must have been designed for both durability and strength. It certainly adds character to the carriage's interior! Those two small bevelled mirrors situated below the luggage racks will come in handy for me to adjust my beret."

The soldier shook his head in disbelief, as he declared, "This is not a second-class carriage, goodness me, no! Its' a sodding first-class one. Bloody hell, mate, you are travelling in frigging style today. How the devil did I manage to afford a first-class ticket, on a frigging soldier's pay? Good grief, what the hell is going on here, then?"

The soldier shook his head from side-to-side and said out loud,

"Blimey, more like a bloody officer's carriage. Maybe someone gave me their ticket by mistake! If only I could remember how I got here!"

He looked away from the interior of the carriage to assess his own attire, as the contrast in quality, style and condition was just too weird for his mind to comprehend.

"Here I am, wearing a post-British WWII khaki uniform, so worn, almost thread-bear, especially at the knees and elbows. Smelling dreadfully sweaty, blood-stained and with a lingering, deathly body odour."

Those strange lingering smells were distasteful, as they entered his nostrils and reminded him of his fallen comrades' bodies lying in the heat of the desert sun. His legs suddenly felt like lead, tight, and cramped, so he lay down to rest, while he whimpered,

"Just for a moment, I'll shut my eyes, just for a moment."

For that soldier, time had no meaning, and he opened his eyes once more and shuffled his weary body and moved his tired legs off the seat onto the floor.

He sat awkwardly perched on the edge of the quaint, upholstered leather seat, the mustiness reminded him of a deathbed.

He wrung his hands, for the feeling of despair overwhelmed the soldier, as he cried out, "Come to your senses, Thomas! You are stronger than this. Pull yourself together. Remember, you are an active serving soldier for goodness sake. Get a grip!"

It had been three years since this soldier had begun his national service in the R.A.O.C. After he had passed his paratrooper training with 'flying colours', Thomas was attached to the 16th Independent Parachute Brigade.

While he served his time in Egypt, he was permitted to wear his Silver Wings. He dreamed every night of home, his beloved Black Greyhound, called Gyp, and his prize-winning 'Homing Pigeons' that had earned him many free pints of Old Tom Ale at his local pub called the Queen's Arms.

The daydreaming ended sharply when suddenly that train jerked to a final standstill within the station. The tired soldier was stretched out upon one of the red leather seats, fast asleep, until the rattling of the steam engine's brakes squealed and woke him up.

The lonely soldier opened his puffy, tired eyes, as if from an extended dream-like state. He looked around somewhat precariously, due to his bewilderment, stretched his quaking, weary legs and realised he had no sense of feeling below his chest. He immediately cried out, "I feel like bloody death and my body is as cold as ice."

The soldier stood up, bent his torso slightly, so both his hands were free to massage his thighs. He proceeded to gently thump his posterior with the knuckles of his clenched fists as he had hoped to bring back life into his frozen body. Eventually, he managed to put one foot in front of the other and forced his stiff legs to walk. He whispered self-encouragement,

"Just two feet, from the carriage seat to the door. Come on, you can do it."

He then used the right sleeve of his khaki jacket, and wiped away a thin covering of red sand from the carriage's glass window. As the glass was still thick with grime, his vision and perception of the people standing directly in front of his carriage was restricted.

He rolled down the dirty window to get a better view, grabbed hold of the red, roller blind's cord and pulled it upwards.

Moving a lever situated at the bottom section of the window, he forced it downwards, which required all his strength. The top glass section of the window dropped down with a loud bang and sat on top of the bottom half of the glass.

"Blimey, it's been a while since this window opened, it's as tight as a duck's arse," he said as he laughed.

The soldier took in a spontaneous deep breath, even though the foul smoke from the carriage's engine drifted inside his carriage. He gasped after his lungs were finally filled with air – as if for the very first time.

He felt more refreshed, yet slightly light-headed and spluttered. Time itself was insignificant to him when he gazed longingly out of the carriage window, he blinked several times just to check that what he saw, was indeed real.

The confused soldier groaned, "Blimey, I must have journeyed far. I thought for a minute I would not have made it back home. I thought I was a goner for a minute back there!"

To check his eyesight had not played a trick on him, with his right hand, he fumbled into his left trouser pocket, pulled out his khaki handkerchief, folded it into a triangle shape; then spat on the top corner. He then gently, wiped his dry eyes and moistened, and cleaned them. Minute particles of fine red sand were left upon his handkerchief,

"That's better – my eyes felt glued together. At least now I can see a little more clearly," he muttered.

The bewildered soldier again blinked several times, to reassure himself that the old railway station was indeed still there, and it was not his imagination that had tricked him.

"Yes, it is there," he cried out emotionally.

The soldier's post-WWII khaki army uniform, was indeed worn, faded, and strangely covered with a residue of red sand particles which dropped onto the floor of the carriage as the soldier moved around. He shuffled his tired, rigid legs off the carriage seat onto the floor and perched himself awkwardly on the edge of the seat anxiously.

"Now, it is time to wait and see what happens next," he declared.

The soldier smiled when the realisation that his long-awaited quest was about to begin. That notion filled him with both excitement and trepidation.

"As I understand it, I have been sent here to complete a mission – a kind of quest, which must be significant; yet the details are not at all clear to me. Guess, I must 'keep the faith', put my trust in God, and allow him to guide me, on whatever path he intends me to take. I trust you to guide me, Lord. Amen," he prayed.

Nevertheless, the soldier's mind was incoherent, mostly because his sense of loneliness hung over him like a shroud, which reinforced his feeling of helplessness.

Unquestionably, he did understand that he was at the mercy of his obligations, which demanded complete obedience from him. The committed soldier understood his quest would undoubtedly unfold, as time went by.

To show his devotion, he bowed his head down, kneeled, and prayed, "Show me the way, O' Lord. Please, give me the strength to carry out my task. Amen."

After he said that prayer, his mind seemed more contented and he remembered his school days. In his mind's eye, he saw children in his old junior school, who received religious studies from their local priest.

Religious studies were the constant factor in his upbringing, and he enjoyed listening to stories from the Bible, as he found them morally reassuring.

He remembered being given a small Bible, after being sworn into the army, along with his pay book. He laughed as he recalled his grandfather's old army tales, "Apparently, soldiers' in the two World Wars, often ran out of toilet paper, so they tore pages from their pay books," and he laughed as he re-called his grandad's story,

"To wipe their arses on."

He re-gained his composure before saying, "Not that any Christian soldier would ever dream of tearing out a page from their Bible, totally unthinkable! But, as many deployed men overseas never expected to return home alive in those times, soldiers saw their pay books as dispensable!"

That memory brought a smile to his face, because he understood no one was ever truly alone – if they kept the faith. He felt sure he would be guided in his quest and his prayers would help him to overcome his fearful loneliness.

The soldier spoke softly when he said, "Faith is a wonderful thing; it allows us to find our inner strength when all else fails us."

The soldier decided to check the theory out, when he placed his right hand into his trouser pocket, he checked to see if his pay book was in there. "Yes!" He cried out. For his small leather-bound pay book was still there. Thomas opened and scrutinised it.

"No pages missing, we must have been lucky," he cried out and laughed loudly.

His pay book was indeed intact, not a page missing, but just a little worse for wear.

"Seems I was luckier than those poor sods that Dad told me about. Nor is there a bullet hole there. Thank God! I wonder if the army owes me any money. Maybe I should check that out; when I have more time," he chuckled, as his thoughts and memories turned to his past life back home.

Happy Memories

Home was where this soldier's parents lived, and his beloved homing pigeons were situated located. Pigeons – which he had reared himself from the best Champion racing pigeons which he had registered with the National Pigeon Club.

His most beloved racing pigeon had been named the Weymouth Hen, and she was indeed his best racer and top flyer. She was so reliable as a fast flier, that his friends persuaded him to enter her for the Weymouth Pigeon Race; a prestigious race in the Pigeon Club Calendar. He remembered how all the local Homing Pigeons, were collected the night before the race began, and were transported by train in large sealed, wicker baskets down to Weymouth town. Once the released pigeons in the race had returned to their home, they were 'clocked-in' by their owners; to make their arrival official.

Thomas's pigeon was the first pigeon which had returned home and should have won the race – had he bothered to 'clock-in' his returning hen. Everyone knew that returning birds needed to be officially clocked-in; to register their arrival back into their relevant pigeon loft. But he could not be bothered to go to his nearest clock-in centre, after he had found his metre damaged. As a result, he lost that chance to win that revered race, and the prestigious opportunity of having gained that year's Official Cup.

He remembered it all as if it were yesterday! "I noted down the arrival time of my beloved Weymouth Hen and showed it later in the day, to my fellow members of the local pigeon club."

He lived at that time with his old granny, so she had taken photos of the Weymouth Hen for posterity; with her old brownie box camera. Just to check if that old photograph of his Weymouth Hen was still on his person, he removed his wallet from his pocket and fumbled through it, and much to his relief pulled out his revered photograph,

'Would you look at that! So glad I decided to take that photo with me to Egypt. Being able to look at that photo always made me feel less homesick', he pondered on that thought for a moment.

In the excitement of having arrived home, he said,

"I wonder how my old village mates are getting on these days. Perhaps, I will be allowed to see them and my beloved pigeons again very soon? I hope so, as that would be great."

He feared that such a meeting would not happen, although his heart was ever hopeful!

He so loved his beloved Weymouth Hen, and if she had won that cup, it would have brought him prestige within the pigeon racing community.

Thomas knew he had acted silly and was disgusted at his laziness, so much so, that he spent the rest of that night in the local pub and drowned his sorrows.

"Good grief, I downed a few pints of ale that particular night with my mates and ended up as 'drunk as a skunk'. Just because, I was lazy! My Weymouth Hen and the local Club were both let-down that day, and I never managed to win another race after that. What a sorrowful affair."

With a big sigh of regret, he shook his head, and said, "'Least my mates rallied around and bought me a few pints of ale to drown my sorrows. I cannot, for the life of me, remember how the bloody hell I got home that night. All I remember is the next morning, I was found fast asleep in my granny's old shed at the side of her house. Oh well, I must have enjoyed myself! I remember, too, having a sore throat, from smoking too many hand-rolled ciggies and having the mother of all headaches."

Home Once More

Thomas was finally about to step onto home ground once more, and he sighed with relief that his quest was finally about to begin.

"This is real," he hesitated for a moment then muttered, "I am not dreaming anymore."

His body quivered momentarily, as a pang of nostalgia passed through his whole body, which made him shiver uncontrollably.

Simultaneously, the railway carriage jerked forward once more, which brought it to a sudden stop, in correct alignment with the platform adjacent to the waiting room. A crowd of passengers were congregated together, where they waited for their early morning train and many stood directly in front of the soldier's carriage.

The soldier was excited to see so many people close by and decided to introduce himself.

"My name is Thomas," he cried out in his excitement, hoping someone would answer him, but no one heard his greeting. Not to be put-off, he whispered, "I am a proud soldier, and I can do this."

Thomas was filled with excitement and joy, as it seemed to him that it was his time to shine – just, one more time.

He shouted out to catch a porter's eye.

"Those chimneys could do with a bit of rendering; the smoke is coming from the sides of that left chimney. Not much has changed since I was last here."

Thomas smiled which lit up his blue eyes until they sparkled.

"Nice to be home once more," said Thomas, with a gentle nod of his head.

The soldier's mind was now focused upon his beloved mother, who he longed to see, and he remembered that he had sent her an ice-blue coloured ladies' handkerchief, which he had purchased from a souvenir shop in his local NAAFI.

He had thought his mum would love such a handkerchief, with its pink, sky-blue and white silk intermingled along the edging and depicted the airborne badge sewn in grey, silk threads upon a light red background in the middle.

He had wondered if his mother placed the silk handkerchief in her treasure box, as she did when given gifts that were precious to her – for safe-keeping. In his euphoria, he shouted in hope that she could hear him,

"I am sure you did put the hanky with your other treasures, after you wrapped it carefully in tissue paper. Remember, Mum, you promised me, you would keep it safe until I returned home. Can you hear me, Mum? I'm on my way, it will not be long now before we are together once more!"

Thomas retrieved his folded red beret from his left pocket and proceeded to slide it onto his head. Carefully, he folded a crease, which he aligned over his right eye.

He then turned his head from side to side, and checked his reflection in the mirror, but an obscure image looked back at him. When he smiled softly at the blurred reflection, he was pleased and declared, "Such a shame I did not have time to clean my beloved Silver Wings," he sighed momentarily. "If only I had been given more time to prepare, but there never is enough time," he said to himself.

His blurry, reflected image looked back at him with approval!

While the soldier pondered his situation, the crowd of people on Platform 1 had dispersed, many towards the waiting room and several people to the toilets. Only a couple of young women were left on that platform and they stood right next to Thomas's carriage. Yet those girls paid no attention to his railway carriage, and their lack of awareness mystified Thomas.

Thomas admired their youthful, glowing beauty, they made him feel alive, he decided to give them a long, suggestive wink. They did not respond, even with his endearing 'come on' smile, they looked straight through him!

"Oh, well, they are not my type," he mumbled and shrugged his shoulders. "They don't know what they are missing, ignoring a handsome chap like me," he said, a little louder, hoping once more that one of those girls would hear him.

His gestures were in vain and ignored. He tried once more to catch their attention, "Hello, pretty ladies, my name is Thomas."

They did not reply, nor even acknowledge his sudden outburst, which made him blush with embarrassment.

He removed his beret from his head and leaned out of the carriage window, as he had hoped that they would have seen his face more clearly and acknowledged him.

"Hey, nice to meet you. How are you doing, pretty ladies?"

They did not answer, so he withdrew his head back into the carriage, replaced his beret and waited.

Thomas was a young man whose tanned, baby face sat comfortably on his broad shoulders, and he gave the impression of a man who, throughout his youth, worked in heavy manual labour because his upper arm muscles were pinched within the sleeves of his jacket.

His body was lean and supple in build, with sun-kissed blond hair that had been shaved so short when he first joined the British Army, the shape of his head shone through like a halo. His eyes were as blue as the Mediterranean Sea, which sparkled, despite the dark circles that framed them. He was of average height and build, except for the uniform he wore which was out of time and place.

Thomas was not easily put off by girls, he decided that there would be plenty of time,

I will wait until I am in the village again for someone is bound to remember me, and there'll be plenty of pretty girls around.

Never one to be snubbed easily, nor put off by stand-offish girls, he thought that once those local girls noticed his distinctive silver badge, pinned strategically in the centre of his red beret, they would swarm around him, and he confidently expressed, "They will soon change their minds – all girls are supposed to love a man in uniform."

Thomas's mind linked back to his love of army life, which denoted his extended family, which meant he felt a part of something splendidly distinguished.

He was a proud, young man, whose intention was to stay in the army as a 'regular' after his national service expired, and he wanted to be part of the Paras for life.

He knew that his silver badge denoted he belonged to the Parachute Regiment, which he wanted everyone to see.

"My cap and my silver wings mean everything to me, far more valuable to me than a few silly girls," he said.

Well, that is how Thomas felt because every time he set his eyes on those beautiful angelic wings, he was filled with pride.

"It is such an honour to be a Para, and every time I touch my silver wings, my heart is filled with joy and seems to miss a beat," he said.

Thomas's confident manner returned, "Time to let all those pretty village girls see that I am now a paratrooper, and I've got my wings to prove it. Those village girls will not be able to take their eyes off me. Maybe I will get a hero's welcome."

So, Thomas stood up straight, replaced his beret and re-adjusted it – and made sure the crease was in the correct position.

"To be sure, you are looking good, Thomas," he said, with a big grin on his face.

Thomas turned his body slightly and checked his image in the carriage's bevelled mirror, for he felt anxious and somewhat nervous. He smiled at his reflected image, gave himself a cheeky wink and murmured to himself, "Thomas, you are quite a handsome young lad. Yes, you've still got your looks." He smiled softly at his image that reflected back at him. "Such a shame I never had time to clean my beloved silver wings," he sighed softly.

Then he cried out, "If only there had been more time!"

Thomas decided to pick up his scattered belongings one by one after he noticed them strewn across the red, plush leather seats and every movement the soldier made enhanced the strong smell of mustiness to that foul air, which overwhelmed him.

"Alright, time to get myself organised. This train will not wait for my departure indefinitely."

Firstly, he leaned forward and picked up the creased, old *Chronicle Newspaper* that was the last gift from home that his sister, June, had sent him. It meant a great deal to him, to be able to read all the local news. Egypt was such a long way from home, he could not have left it behind.

Next, a brown, tubular-shaped leather case caught his eye. With great care, his right hand picked up its long, folded-over shoulder strap; as it was quite fragile. He opened the case, gently, pulled out a long, rolled-up mission map and as he un-rolled the map, silent, salty tears rolled down his cheeks, stung his lips and eventually dropped down onto his uniform jacket.

Once the map was entirely stretched-out before him, Thomas noticed a targeted area circled upon the map in red ink.

"Or is that blood?" he asked himself. "Too late to worry about that coincidental fact now," he cried.

The map left him spellbound as the inclination to touch that red circle overpowered him because it awakened his senses. With his fingertips, he followed the outline of the red circle with caution. The hairs on his head stood on end. Those stinging tears were profuse, and it seemed futile to have wiped them away. His lips quivered, as a lump of fear filled his throat and almost choked him.

Something strange overpowered the soldier's vision as his senses became numb. He drifted into an out of body experience, his sense of time and space diminished, his mind battled to conquer that phenomenon.

Nevertheless, he perceived his physical body from above, as his spirit continued to float upwards, higher, and higher towards an intense, bright light.

Without warning, his spiritual being was united into his physical body. Immediately, he experienced extreme pain and as the pain increased, he blacked out.

Enlightenment

Thomas lay down motionless, frozen with fright, his emotions had overpowered his senses. The stench of warm blood filled his nostrils and it alarmed his taste buds when the blood trickled down the back of his throat, burned as it entered his lungs and choked the life out of him.

An evil shadow cast over the soldier, left him rigid with fear, as his legs finally gave way and he collapsed in a ruck onto the cold, carriage floor.

At this point an event occurred, which might have been defined as miraculous and initiated the soldier's enlightenment. A blinding ball of light appeared in the sky outside. That dazzling beam settled over the soldier's carriage, yet people in the station remained oblivious.

Furthermore, that mysterious phenomenon intensified, formed into a shaft of light, entered the carriage through its open window and encircled the soldier's body. Finally, it settled in the form of a halo over the soldier's face momentarily, then took the shape of an angel of the highest order.

The presence of that radiant, spiritual being, dissipated the darkness; which held the soldier captive through his self-doubt.

That angelic messenger glowed when its warm wings embraced the soldier and dispersed light particles when it hovered over Thomas's face, before it entered his body. When the soldier awoke from his deathly state he was confused because when Thomas's eyes slowly opened, his former dizziness and pain were healed. He rose from the floor and stood up straight as his strength was renewed.

When the soldier saw his reflection in the mirror, he noticed that his tears appeared to have given his cheeks a glow, and he felt quite vigorous. He proceeded to unbutton his khaki jacket, followed by his shirt and as if by magic, the wounds which had pained him so much after those fatal bullets had entered his body, were healed. Not even a scar remained, so he closed his eyes and looked upwards and gave thanks to his God,

"Thank you, Lord, thank you!"

As if in answer to his cry of thanks, he walked over to the carriage window, looked at the sky, where his eyes were instinctively drawn towards the East and he noticed, "A double rainbow! Now, that is a joyful sight to behold, a good omen indeed," he said.

His face glowed with delight as his body tingled with pure joy and excitement, and he clapped his hands with glee.

Faith and Family Attachments

Thomas, like most children of his generation, grew up in a close community, where religion played its part through regular Sunday Church attendance and morning services; which took place before School registration began. Thomas was not overly religious, but he knew 'right from wrong' due to his religious upbringing.

Consequently, Thomas immediately understood that he had experienced a blessing and as such, the challenges which lay ahead were for a purpose; he knew that he must face them, if his quest was to be fulfilled.

Indeed, he perceived his quest as a test of his faith and honour, not only as a soldier but that of a son; determined to prove that his heart was indeed full of selfless love.

He needed to show his devotion to his mother's welfare after she cried out to him, while in the depths of despair. He heard her disembodied voice from afar and his love for her, overpowered his own need to rest in peace.

Thomas had only two photographs in his wallet, one of his beloved mother, and the other of his little baby sister. The first time he met his youngest sister, was when she was in his mother's arms in the maternity hospital shortly after being born. Thomas was overwhelmed by his sister's beautiful, deep blue eyes, enhanced by her pink cheeks which glowed and her white blonde curly hair; and he had nicknamed her Pinky.

He knew his departure from England was imminent so, his mother allowed him to cradle Pinky. His baby sister looked directly at him and smiled – not any old smile but the kind of smile which linked two souls' future intrinsically.

He remembered wondering whether he and this little bundle of joy would ever meet again; and if so, would she remember him. He was about to be deployed with his army regiment to Egypt. He knew that a soldier's life was a precarious one, with no guarantees of survival!

Nevertheless, his last happy memory of being able to hold 'new life' in his arms stayed with him. He held on to that treasured feeling when times were hard and unpredictable; while he served in the Middle East.

"Yes, my sister's photograph always managed to put a smile on my face," he said in an orotund voice.

Thomas's inbuilt sense of duty towards his mother and baby sister overrode any personal needs, because he had sensed the future welfare of his beloved sister, depended upon the survival of their mother.

The soldier's left hand trembled as he took his wallet from his trousers' left back pocket and retrieved two old photographs, and remembered how he wrote to his mother and asked her,

'Please Mother, send me an up-to-date photograph of our Pinky, as the old one got torn, and make sure it is a good one! My mates here cannot believe that I have a baby sister with such beautiful blue eyes. Do not forget, make it soon. Your ever-loving son, Thomas.'

He looked upon his sister's photograph once more and smiled, and in a wobbly voice, cried out,

"Don't worry, little one, Tommy is going to make sure you are all right!"

Reminiscence

Thomas knew he had accomplished his last mission in Egypt to the best of his abilities, he remembered his comrades-in-arms say so, as he lay wounded inside his military Land Rover. It had happened quickly, as a fellow soldier entered the vehicle, the safety-catch on his machine-gun released and the gun fired bullets continuously into Thomas's chest.

"It was an accident. No one was to blame, just bad fate. It must have been my time and all I ask of my fellow soldiers is that you remember me. Remember me, please," he cried out, to the ghostly listeners of his past life.

Thomas, the paratrooper, had been formally trained as an army driver, so he was one of the three army Land Rover drivers when the incident happened.

Thomas remembered that day's mission, even from the point from which the sun rose in the East that morning.

His orders were to pick up stragglers waiting near a village, situated only a couple of miles outside his army camp.

Thomas was one of the allocated drivers in a three-vehicle convoy mission and his mates were equipped with both light rifles and semi-automatics. Although the day went well, navigation around the designated areas was prone to problems due to the intransigent local hostility; nevertheless, the mission was completed, despite the intervention of fate.

Thomas pleaded to his ghostly listeners, "Why the bloody hell did that have to happen?"

Thomas shook his head in disbelief of his present circumstances as he cried out in anger,

"Shit! Talk about being in bloody limbo, I am too young to die. Is it too late? Bollocks!" he screamed at the top of his voice.

Then, with pale, cold hands, he opened his battered old suitcase, looked towards his precious journal, telescope, newspaper and with prudence, he picked up his treasured mementoes one by one, and placed them carefully inside his suitcase.

Although his suitcase was quite small, it was sturdy, with a hand-stitched leather handle at the top and was embellished with brass security hinges on all four corners. Thomas took his time, for he believed that such tasks should be completed with diligence; primarily, as that suitcase had belonged to his father and it was the final gift he received from him before leaving home to join the British Army. Mumbling, he said, 'Of course, my dad's gift was not new, because no way could any low-income family have afforded to buy luxuries.' He had received his gift with gratitude. And, continued, 'No doubt initially it was purchased from the local pawn broker's shop, and that meant that some poor sod had to trade the suitcase in, to pay a bill.'

Thomas loved his old suitcase and had kept it with him throughout his travels, with his mementoes inside. Whereas his army kitbag was filled with his general everyday army clothing, equipment, and general sundries. He pondered, 'Although my suitcase is a standard style and slightly battered, the brass hinges helped it to stand the test of time,' "Thanks, Dad, this suitcase suits me just fine," he said out loud.

The soldier moved slowly around and while doing so, caught a disjointed reflection of himself in the carriage's bevelled mirrors. It amused him, and he laughed out loud at his own weird image.

That distorted image reminded him of a visit to a 'Hall of Mirrors' during a visit to a circus as a child. The more the soldier stared at his distorted image, his body chilled right down to his bones, so he turned away!

Thomas felt perplexed, yet, after he took several deep breaths, straightened up his shoulders, took more deep breaths; his nerves steadied and with guttural sounds, he blurted out, "Right, Thomas, let us do this then and do it right, for she deserves a good send-off."

Nevertheless, Thomas's senses were on overload when he felt a dreadful feeling of foreboding and he trembled from a different kind of fear that he had not felt before; not even in battle, and he shivered from head to toe.

The soldier's mind continued to slip back in time, and he remembered his arrival at Euston Station, London, when his regiment was about to embark for Suez, Egypt.

Tommy, as his comrades had nicknamed him while serving with the 16 Independent Parachute Brigade Group in the 1950s, loved the army.

He wrote letters to his mum back home, discussed his future, as he knew his mum would have preferred him to have returned home, where he would be safe. His mother had hoped that after his National Service was completed, he would get himself a job, as a mechanic, in a local garage. Her words rang in his ears, 'Build a good life for yourself son, find a nice local girl and settle-down. I miss you.'

Nevertheless, the notion of remaining as a career-soldier with the Paras was his ambition, and with pride he said aloud, "I can think of nothing I would have loved more than to have served with the Airborne Forces for life!"

He was not afraid of becoming a combat soldier! Excited – yes, at the prospect of his regiment experiencing a 'little action'. He, like his fellow comrades, were fed-up with hanging around his Catterick barracks, and when his basic training ended, he felt restless.

On arrival, at Euston Station, a photographer approached a group of soldiers from his regiment and despite having been told to "piss off and do one!", the photographer took photographs of them all – without their permission; then demanded they pay him, two shillings for each picture. They had refused to pay the photographer until he threatened,

"I'll report you to the police, you little gits."

The photographer knew the soldiers could not afford to get into any trouble with the police, and when Thomas's soldier companion declared, "I'm skint, mate. Can you pay for mine?"

Thomas removed his wallet from his top jacket pocket, and at that precise moment, the photographer clicked his lens and he found himself too, tricked into the scam.

Fate had played its hand with Thomas, as that photograph turned out to be the only one ever taken of him in full uniform, before his embarkation to Egypt. He posted that last memento to his beloved mum, as he knew she would treasure the photograph and it would be a keepsake memory of him.

"Maybe, she will think of me from time to time. Oh, I hope so," he remembered saying to his fellow soldiers.

Thomas's first and last day in London was portrayed with his hands on his wallet, and a grim, angry look on his face. A photographic record of Thomas's 'run-in' with that photographer before boarding the train for Dover. That story was passed through Thomas's family from generation to generation, as another instance of his 'run of bad luck'.

It seemed a long time, Thomas thought, 'since I have enjoyed the privilege, of seeing my reflection looking right back at me.' So, he stood proud when he said,

"Right, Thomas, let's do this then and do it right, for she deserves a proper send-off," But, it was whispered – as not to be overheard. Nevertheless, an intense glow of excitement rushed through his confused mind,

"Strange," he muttered.

Thomas's mind wandered backwards to Egypt, as he visualised that other place, where mirrors, general toiletries and especially water were a luxury.

He saw past events, in a blurred, confused, and sparse manner, which made them difficult to comprehend. He felt that he had become the perceiver of his life's journey and groaned, "That sodding red sand seemed to embed in one's bloody skin – let alone my kit, and it never really washed out."

He shook his head in disbelief of how he managed to complete all his daily ablutions, and laughed as he cried out,

"Bloody hell! We spent too much of our spare time washing our kit with Carbolic soap in scummy water. Our trousers dried as hard as cardboard in that desert heat."

Childhood Adventures

In contrast to Thomas's desert experience, that poor, English country lad grew up where water was a natural resource – which was plentiful; especially as his village was almost encircled by tributaries of a significant river, called the River Weaver. It was in that local river that he had learnt to swim. 'Tommy boy', as his school friends called him, gathered together with his school pals at every given opportunity and enjoyed swimming throughout their summer holidays; an experience which he never forgot.

Indeed, everyone from Thomas's village congregated around that local River at weekends and throughout those summer months. Families' from his village attended their church or chapel services, then headed for the local picnic spots beside the river; with their picnic boxes, which were filled with homemade treats.

Old, rolled-up blankets were draped around the women's shoulders and when they reached their picnic destination; the blankets were used as tablecloths. and each family group sat down around the edges of their make-do tablecloths.

Several children carried cushions for their parents, who sat upon them. Once the picnic baskets were opened up, the homemade treats were placed in the centre of those old woollen blankets. Children sat around and waited for their parents to give permission, for them to tuck in, and enjoy their mother's homemade treats.

Thomas remembered that he loved all the food on offer, but mainly his granny's homemade fruit loaf smothered with farm butter. That delightful memory made him drool, having remembered such a pleasant childhood memory.

"I can almost taste all those flavours, which were within Gran's cake, even now!" said Thomas.

Thomas also recalled villagers congregated together to share their cars with their friends, but those who were not offered a lift in their neighbour's car, took a shortcut to the local picnic spot on foot through the local farmer's fields.

There was always a rush for people to find the best picnic spots around, which were situated as close as possible to the local mill. It was a mill that had stood for nearly a century, next to the River Weaver. It was quite a competition, to be the first family to arrive at that local picnic spot.

Thomas remembered, "'It's the early bird that catches the worm,' as me old dad used to say."

Therefore, in his mind's eye, a summer scene appeared before his eyes, where grownups speedily opened their picnic hampers, placed the food in the centre of their blanket, tablecloths and sat in idleness upon cushions, and chatted away, while they watched their children play. The sound of laughter filled Thomas's ears and the smell of freshly baked bread, baked ham shanks, homemade honey and fruit cakes, and mugs of beer tantalised his taste buds.

"Blimey, what would I give now for a pint of beer," he said. He remembered,

"Most people back then who intended to swim in the river, went prepared, by wearing their swimming costumes or trunks under their regular clothing; as it saved time and the embarrassment; of having to strip off their outer garments in public. No one wanted to get caught in public with their pants down."

The old mill overlooked the river and had several giant 'overflow' culverts. Those culverts allowed excess floodwater within the mill pond to pass beneath the mill and into the river.

Nevertheless, during the summertime, those mill culverts were usually 'high and dry'. The women and girls took advantage of those dry culverts to dry themselves off, after swimming in the river. It was 'out of bounds' for the men and boys. Thomas's face wore a smirk, as he said aloud, "'Boys will be boys', as the old saying goes."

Thomas remembered how the older boys used to sneak around the entrance to the girl's changing area, teased and peeked at them, from the land above.

The boys quickly dispersed when the older women threatened them, "We'll give you lads a damn good thrashing when we come out of here, if you little devils do not go away."

Eventually, the boys admired the girls from a safe distance and waited until the girls' reappeared from the culverts, dressed in their sundresses, or shorts and tops.

Apart from swimming, Thomas and his teenage mates loved to watch the girls stretched out, sunbathing on the banks of the river, but many of the boys received a 'clip across the ear', or a 'kick up the backside' from an angry big brother or annoyed father. 'Only idiots got caught,' he mused.

Thomas's face glowed with delight, as he recollected the rules of the day for the changing areas, "Boys and men to the left, girls and women to the right."

The riverbank areas were well-trodden down by the farmer's cattle, which made them safe places for the younger children; who played or paddled around the sandbanks. Sunbeams danced across the water and Thomas remembered how the youngest children giggled and shouted out with glee.

He remembered too that many of the children's parents placed inner tubes saved from old car tyres over their children's heads, instead of buying expensive 'water wings'.

Thomas saw all those happy childhood memories with his 'mind's eye' and it pleased him to say,

"You don't need money to enjoy yourself when one has good friends for company. I am still a country lad at heart, no one can take away those happy memories from me. I thank God, that we were so innocent in those days, that we just enjoyed our summer holidays with those we loved. No regrets," he mumbled.

Thomas was determined to set his mind on happy elements from his childhood and dismissed the darker memories. Just the same, he understood why grownups set rules, "For our safety and everyone looked after each other in those days, and the main rule was that,' You only swim in safe areas – even if adults are present.' Thomas, like many of his

41

school pals, often stayed too long in the water without taking breaks on land to warm themselves. The river was ice cold, but they only came out of the water, when yelled at by their family,

"Come on, out of there, time to eat something."

Before the sun had set, everyone had left the water, changed back into their Sunday clothes. Fussing mothers passed around warm cardigans and jumpers while they continued supervising their family picnic, but by dusk, families headed for home. It was a time when everyone congregated together to socialise as a community, celebrated friendship, and companionship.

Thomas's community had come through two World Wars together, welcomed POWs that had stayed after the wars and many foreign soldiers had married local girls, and settled in the village.

Thomas knew his village community was friendly, caring, and open minded to new ideas, while they tried to hold onto their trusted, and valued traditions,

"I remember how my brother, Ned, saved a girl's life once," he whispered to his silent listeners. "She had found herself in trouble, after swimming too close to a whirlpool; which was hidden by overgrown trees. Bloody hell! He was brave and a much stronger swimmer than me." After a moment of thought, he continued to say, "We really looked after each other in those days."

Obliviousness

No one took any notice of the arrival of that unscheduled steam train next to Platform 1, or the fact that it only had one solitary passenger, despite his strange appearance.

Consequently, when Thomas rolled down the window of his carriage, opened the door and departed from that train in a gingerly manner, and stepped onto that grey, cold, concrete platform, no one acknowledged him.

That solitary, lonely passenger wore a post WWII British khaki uniform, red beret with a silver winged badge- pinned to its centre front. The soldier's heavily laced-up, leather army boots had a sprinkling of red sand, which fell from his boots, as he moved and dispersed upon the concrete flooring and strangely-left a faint imprint of his footprint- for posterity.

The bemused, British soldier carried a battered old leather suitcase in his left hand. A khaki kitbag, drawn together at the top with string-cord with looped ends; held tightly within the four finger of the soldier's right hand. The soldier's 'grip of death' resulted in his transparent hands and knuckles, portraying his tenseness.

The soldier's uniform was embellished with shiny brass buttons situated on each of the two top pockets of his tightly fitted jacket. Two more buttons held the sleeve cuffs together and several more were down the front lapel. Only the collar of his green shirt, along with matching tie, were visible from within the jacket, completed by a canvas belt that had a shiny brass fastening. Thomas's trouser hems were held tightly together by heavy canvas spats that covered his instep and ankle, and black leather, heavily laced-up army boots completed his uniformed outfit.

Thomas's pride and joy of course were the red beret set off by his silver wings. Therefore, the overall impression should have been, to those waiting passengers on Platform 1; that of a soldier, who had returned from a long deployment overseas.

Thomas stood firmly on the dirty, old concrete platform with his feet in the 'at ease' position, just as if he were back on the parade ground, under the order of his RSM.

His body quivered when the reality of his predicament struck him," I have finally arrived home." He said.

Although Thomas understood the purpose of his unforeseen premature return home, the journey itself was still a mental blank.

Thomas's journey through time and space, was meant to be unpredictable and was not guaranteed, to end well. Thomas was determined to face his fears and take charge of his destiny, but with anger in his voice, he stated,

"Alright, God, I accept I'm under new orders, but I do not like it!"

Anger quickly turned to joy, due to his understanding that he had been given a chance to put things right, before it was too late.

His confidence returned when he realised his quest was about to begin, so Thomas spoke out loudly, for everyone to hear,

"Born here and yet –" he paused, as a silent, salty, solitary tear glided softly down his right cheek and into his mouth, and in doing so, took his breath away. He swallowed deeply, regained his composure, and inhaled deeply before he said,

"I don't seem to recognise this place. These people, who look straight ahead but not at me. Where am I, if I am not home?" he cried, penitently.

No one heard the soldier's plea, no one looked his way – no one rebuked him. People just went about their business.

Thomas's legs shook but with a longing in his heart, he walked over towards the waiting room, and because there were several waiting passengers in his way; he completed the old military manoeuvre of 'changing step', so as not to bump into anyone.

The soldier turned his head back slightly – momentarily, he gazed longingly, at the women who stood quite close to him and mumbled to himself,

"My, oh my! How the fashions have changed since I was last home. Skirts have got a lot shorter," he declared. Thomas glanced at the girl's slim legs, and his heart rejoiced when he said,

"Guess, I'm just a 'lady's man', and why not!"

Suddenly, passengers rushed out of the waiting room and congregated onto Platform 1. Thomas dodged the rush and ventured towards the waiting room door.

Thomas's legs shook when a pang of loneliness overcame him, filled his heart with sadness; he wanted to talk to someone – anyone would do!

"How lonely can a chap feel before someone takes pity on him and opens up, to have a friendly conversation. Surely, there will be someone inside who is willing to have a conversation with me," he agonised.

Thomas placed his right hand on the waiting room's shiny, brass doorknob and tentatively turned the knob to the right, and the door opened. Slowly, but surely, a sunbeam surrounded his head in the form of a halo. As he moved, the sunbeam shone directly in front of Thomas, which allowed him to see how sparsely furnished the room was. After he had entered the room, he turned around and shut the door behind him – ever so gently, so as not to disturb anyone that might be sitting quietly inside.

The Waiting Room

The first thing which caught Thomas's eye was an ancient, rusty, old cast iron coke stove, which took up most of the far corner of the room opposite the entrance door and he noticed that the fire within it burned brightly.

Thomas set his eyes upon an old railway guardsman who stood to the left of the stove. The man stoked the fire with an iron fire poker, and the soldier watched the embers burst into intense flames.

That lonely soldier watched with delight as that fire crackled and flames engulfed the wooden logs within the stove. Such explosive sounds also reminded him of a machine gun 'firing at will', but he soon overcame that fear.

The soldier ventured closer towards the fire, stretched out his hands towards the intense heat given out and gradually, the coldness of his torso thawed out, and he felt comforted.

The soldier did not understand why the guardsman did not move aside, nor allowed him access to the fire and he was annoyed that the old guardsman did not acknowledge his presence. Yet, the guardsman shuddered from head to toe, when he sensed a cold presence within the room and turned to check if the door had been left open! When the old man replaced the poker down on the floor in front of the stove, he trembled, because he was filled with fear.

The guardsman decided to go and make himself a hot drink, and talked to himself, as 'Oldtimers' often do, "It's chilly in here this morning, or maybe I'm coming down with a cold. Time for a steaming-hot cuppa tea, me old mate. Nowt wrong with, a body talking to himself; so long as you don't answer yourself back. Well, that's what me old mother used to say," and he giggled at his peculiarity.

Thomas smirked when he watched the old guardsman talk to himself and sat his weary body down on a wooden bench, which was situated directly in front of the coke stove. Once settled, he proceeded to rub his hands together, for he had hoped to bring life back into them.

Thomas sat contented upon the old wooden bench in the waiting room and pondered in his mind the irony of his situation. The soldier sat motionless and watched people enter, then leave the room, which helped him to relax.

Time had no meaning, as his mind seemed locked into a dreamscape mode once more. He was not feeling sociable, after he shouted out "Good morning," to each person who had entered the Waiting Room, because, no one bothered to look his way, or replied to his friendly greetings.

It seemed strange to the lonely soldier that there was no one to meet him at the station and his emotional state escalated. The soldier's disappointment quickly angered him, and a rage overcame him, when he shouted out, "Where are they? Surely, they know what time my train was due to arrive?"

Thomas's anger left him dizzy and he leant forward, placed his head in his hands and wept uncontrollably.

Frustrated, he rose to his feet and decided he was going to speak to the railway attendant.

The old guardsman eventually returned to the waiting-room and Thomas noticed he was carrying a large, tin mug cupped in his hands, which contained steaming hot tea. The guardsman embraced his mug of tea and enjoyed each sip of his beverage, totally oblivious of the soldier's presence.

Thomas felt the need to apologise for his temper, "Sorry for the outburst mate, I'm just exhausted – must have been the long journey and I'm so hungry, I cannot remember the last time I ate anything."

Although, the guard stood directly in front of Thomas, he did not acknowledge him. Thomas glared at him for a long time, but the old man did not respond, so he cried out, "Least you could do is offer a veteran a hot brew. Can you hear me? I am talking to you! Why do you not answer me? So, that is the thanks a poor soldier gets for fighting for his king and country? Please your bloody self!"

Thomas rose slowly from his sitting position and paced across the room, like a trapped animal, "Must calm down, must calm down," he mumbled to his agitated self.

Thomas decided to sit back down on the bench and concentrated his mind upon the fire's glowing embers, which had filled the room with intermittent light; which danced around the room, and bounced from wall to wall, and that pleased him.

"I know what I'll do to pass the time; I'll read a copy of the latest newspaper; it'll give me a chance to catch up on what's going on in the village these days."

So, he clumsily reached for a copy of the local *Chronicle* marked 'Archives' on a shelf behind him. He leaned back, opened up the old paper and began to read it page to page, which relaxed him, until he turned to the obituary page.

There, under the surnames of all the deceased, his eyes were fixated upon a name that froze him to the bone, and he shuddered as he cried out,

"No! That is not right; this must be someone playing a sick joke on me, it cannot be true … Is it that late already?"

The soldier's realization left him full of trepidation as he was puzzled as to how his quest was to be completed.

"Now, what am I to do, this is just all too much for me alone!"

Self-doubt made the soldier question whether his fear was cowardice, for he had never thought of himself as a coward!

"Is this isolation another test?" he cried out to his silent listeners.

"Never, not ever, have I feared a challenge before – not even when under fire on missions. I know I'm not perfect – I ask you for goodness' sake, who is?" He dropped his head in shame.

"My dad liked his beer and ciggies, so I never saw such traits as being wrong, and I do have an eye for the ladies. Surely, needing company is not an immoral characteristic? Please, if you are guiding me, Lord, please, do not make me do this alone," he paused and swallowed down hard to suppress his self-doubt.

In hope, he continued his prayer, "This is my first mission on my own, Lord. I do not want to mess it up, so how about sending me a suitable companion – someone more experienced than I. Someone who can 'ground me' and help me focus. Amen."

At that point, the room revolved around Thomas and he was transported into another place, where angels surrounded him, and a bright light engulfed him.

Dare he, should he have presumed that his prayer had been heard?

While in that celestial trance, he was thrust far into the future, where he observed a complex vision of doom.

Thomas felt that God had forewarned him that 'Armageddon' was imminent and he knew he must remain positive if he was to fulfil his quest.

Supernatural Forces

Thomas had been thrust far into the future and found himself an observer of a nuclear war, that was taking place between two Superpowers'. He experienced the 'dark side' of evil forces, that had consumed mankind's minds and filled their thought process with hatred and murderous notions. It pained him to see the war-like mind-set, of those weak-minded humans; who were under the influence of Demons, but he was unable to intervene.

He watched State Leaders, use their economic and political greed, to feed mankind's selfishness for their own selfish desires. Nations formed new alliances with evil dictators and good men's judgement was lost, overwhelmed their common sense, compassion, and tolerance towards their neighbours.

People fell into despair, when food was unevenly distributed and worldwide poverty prevailed, drinking water was polluted and the seas of the world became so contaminated; that all life forms within them died. Hunger and greed encouraged hatred and suspicion between people and rich countries practiced extreme isolationism. An escalation of the 'Arms Race' led mankind into World War III.

During the nuclear winter that followed that war, the destruction of Planet Earth was catastrophic. Human survivors evolved into war-like nomadic tribes, and many tribes turned cannibalistic because all domestic and farm animals were extinct.

Storms raged and encircled the planet for over a hundred years and finally, an evil voracious vortex engulfed the Earth itself. Avenging, Dark Angels emerged from within that vortex. They searched in vain for our angels, on Earth; determined to destroy their spiritual power of goodness.

The sound of silence was a deafening moment on the Earth, as darkness encircled the planet. Angels of Darkness descended upon the Earth. Swirled over the remnants of mankind with harrowing screams and demonic tongues were thrust forth from their mouths – with the vengeance of Satan himself. Dark Angels surrounded the masses, devoured both innocents and sinners alike!

Shortly after, Planet Earth was bombarded by alien spaceships, until no life forms remained; the Earth was left scorched and barren. Only then did the alien demons pull their spaceships out of Earth's orbit and move on, faster than the speed of light, to their next target. Earth teared itself apart from within and exploded, all that remained was remnant particles, which were scattered throughout the universe.

The Reunion

Suddenly, Haven's station's Waiting Room door opened and a figure of a man, slowly emerged out of a dazzling beam of light and walked into the waiting room, waved his right hand at Thomas, who sat rigid in his trance-like state.

The figure looked directly at Thomas, and shouted to rouse the soldier, "Hey, mate, thought you were going to wait for me? That is what was agreed, don't you remember? It took me bloody ages to connect with you."

The visitor's loud voice awakened Thomas, and he looked upwards to see a halo of bright lights that had surrounded the man's outline. Thomas rubbed his eyes, for the light blinded his vision. With squinted eyes, he watched as the emerging figure walked slowly and surely towards him.

Suddenly, Thomas recognised the Royal Marine's face, smiled, and then walked over towards him. The two men embraced each other, and the soldier laughed out loud – almost in a frenzy.

"Well, hello, Uncle Ted, am I glad to meet you at last." Thomas grabbed Ted's right hand and shook it with gusto and continued to say, "Welcome, mate."

Both men stared into each other's eyes, smiled warmly and their eyes filled with tears of joy.

The last time Thomas had seen his uncle's image was on a photograph, which had been sent to him, by his father's brother. The photo portrayed Ted in his British Royal Marine's uniform. It was a memento for Thomas's father, because it had been taken just after Ted joined his shipmates on the Light Battle Cruiser, *The Exeter*, where Ted served as a gunner.

Thomas remembered the 'Battle of The River Plate', which took place off the coast of South America in WWII, from his school's history lessons. It was heart-breaking information for a small child to learn, especially as his beloved uncle died in that famous battle. Apparently, his dad said that his brother was killed instantly, as the guns received a direct hit!

Thomas looked at the striking figure of that marine, who stood directly in front of him. His slim uncle stood tall, handsome and gave the impression still of a young man who oozed with confidence. He proudly admired his uncle's image because he had finally met his childhood hero.

Thomas spoke out, in a lowly and respectful manner to his Uncle Ted,

"I remember you from Dad's photograph, Uncle Ted. You still look smart and proud!"

His uncle acknowledged Thomas with a grimaced grin which made his handsome profile look somewhat taut, like a tight, controlled ship.

Ted's nephew diverted his eyes momentarily from his newly acquired companion and tried to understand the irony of their present situation, which they had found themselves in.

Thomas felt it was ironic that two relatives from different eras in time had been thrown together unexpectedly. After he regained his composure, Thomas's sense of humour returned, and he laughed before he declared to his uncle,

"Born here, Ted, yet I have no idea where I am. How about you?"

Thomas felt dizzy, after he had looked deep into his companion's eyes –searching for answers.

Thomas sat back down on the cold wooden bench again and stated,

"Blimey mate, the room is revolving so fast I feel quite queasy. Are you as hungry as me? I cannot remember the last time I ate any food, can you?"

Ted smiled back at Thomas and sat down beside him to comfort his nephew, placed his arms around Thomas's shoulders, in the form of a manly hug that only deployed soldiers would understand, and the silent gesture spoke volumes!

Thomas lifted up his face and smiled at his uncle, as his friend spoke to him in a gentle, but warning tone,

"Look Thomas, remember, things have changed somewhat since your last visit home. Surely you anticipated that! Are you sure that you still want to do this? It is not too late to turn back, but remember, mate, we only have one chance to gain our wings, so take things slow and easy like!"

Thomas nodded his head in compliance, and both men stood to attention, picked up their kitbags and swung them over their shoulders, as real soldiers do! They then proceeded towards the waiting room door, Ted took the lead and grabbed hold of its doorknob, turned it slowly clockwise, opened it and the sun's warm rays lit up their faces with joy and their souls filled with delight.

Ted took out his cigarette tin and handed his nephew a hand-rolled cigarette, and with an appealing voice asked,

"How's about a ciggie, Thomas?"

When his companion saw the tobacco, his eyes lit up with delight, and he answered,

"You bet, mate. I was gasping for a cigarette."

Thomas placed the cigarette between his dry, red lips and took a long pleasing draw on it after his uncle lit it, using his old silver military lighter.

Ted then proceeded to light himself a cigarette. When the plumes of smoke rose above their heads, they felt more relaxed in each other's company.

"Nothing like a cigarette, mate, when one is feeling down, especially when the moment is shared with a pal. It makes one feel less isolated."

His companion's breathless voice was lost, as he coughed repeatedly, and they both broke out in spontaneous laughter, at their strange predicament.

Ted proclaimed to Thomas,

"You look the spitting image of your dad, with a ciggie in your chops. Some things never change, do they?" They both roared with laughter.

Thomas instinctively understood that his uncle knew all about his fearful vision, so he decided not to mention it!

Marching Orders

Thomas faced his beloved Uncle Ted and saw for himself the joy his uncle was experiencing, after a warm sunbeam lit up his tanned face and teased him when he said,

"Your suntan is extremely dark, compared to my golden tan – how come?"

Ted laughed, then replied, "It is the sea air, lad, which makes us sailors tan so easily."

An agitated Thomas shrugged his shoulders, and insisted, "We must put one foot in front of the other, Uncle Ted."

He felt his beloved uncle was still 'dilly-dallying' so to demand his uncle's attention, Thomas gave his uncle a sharp, decisive order,

"Forward march, soldier!"

Thomas was keen to move forward but paused momentarily, looked directly at Ted's face and made eye contact once more, before he professed loudly, "Hey, mate. You've just received your marching orders."

To which, the marine stood to attention, and respectfully saluted his companion, with a wide grin across his face. Ted was a sailor who had never refused an 'order', so he quickly patted his nephew on the shoulder, and they set off together but not before Thomas shouted to his companion,

"Quick march! Left, right! Come on, sailor, pick those feet up as you're not in the dance hall now!"

Ted gave his nephew a side-glance smirk but followed the given order. No one noticed the khaki-clad soldier or the Royal Marine who marched 'in-step' together; despite their loud voices that echoed throughout the station and no one reacted to their commotion.

Their synchronised footsteps left no impression upon the dirt footpath, when they passed through the old, turn-style railway entrance gate, and stepped out of the Railway Station onto that adjoining cobbled lane.

"Let us sing a jolly hymn, Thomas," declared his uncle.
"How about the hymn,
'Onward Christian Soldiers'?" asked Thomas.
"Good choice, me lad," replied Ted.

They walked on air as they joyfully sang their favourite hymn,
"Onward, Christian Soldiers *Marching as to War,*
With the Cross of Jesus, going on before.
Christ, the Royal Master
Leads against the foe;
Forward into Battle' See,
His banners go!
At the sign of triumph
Satan's host doth flee;
On then, Christian soldiers,
On to Victory.
Hell's foundation's quiver
At the shout of praise;
Brothers, lift your voices'
Loud your anthems raise."

Unexpectedly, Ted raised his hand into the air and said, "Stop, stop! Please stop! I fear we may be too presumptuous!" Thomas was perturbed by his uncle's sudden outburst and stopped in mid-sentence, looked directly at Ted for an explanation.

"What did we do wrong?" he asked.
Ted's grave and fearful expression filled his nephew with trepidation when he asked his companion for an explanation.

"Whatever is going to happen, Uncle Ted? It was just a hymn – unless of course, you know something that you are afraid to tell me."

The marine told his friend what he felt, he 'needed to know'; too much future knowledge would have influenced Thomas's reactions when faced with his real quest.

Ted knew that his prodigy must fulfil his quest by using his own freewill and must not be overly influenced by either himself or additional knowledge that concerned the future of mankind.

Mankind's destiny depended upon Thomas being able to overcome his weaknesses and selfish needs.

The marine's demure stiffened when he said, "Listen carefully to what I have to tell you, Thomas, and when I have finished, you must not question or ask questions; for it is strictly forbidden by a higher force than I."

Thomas listened intensely and instinctively stood 'at ease' as his pal told him, "Right, me lad. It seems to me that you feel that there is only one outcome when this quest of yours ends, and that is one that you desire. Life is never straightforward while we are alive, so why should it change after death! I know you now understand our destiny cannot be changed and if we interfere with the 'Timeline', there is a 'knock-on' effect which can change the future of mankind. Do you understand what I am trying to say, Thomas lad?"

Thomas's eyes were as 'wide as saucers', and the hair on his neck seemed to be alive with electricity, but he answered subserviently,

"You mean I cannot change what has already happened!"

"Yes, in part, Thomas, but you will have to face a personal challenge which, in-turn, will affect the future. You must know what to do – when that time is upon you. Only you alone, must perceive which action to take. In other words, you will have to make a difficult choice, and I just hope you make the right one!"

Thomas's sensibilities were strong, despite his awareness of his imperfections in character. His truthfulness and common sense he knew would help him succeed, and so, he answered positively,

"I understand that you will not help me make that decision then, Ted?"

Ted replied, "No lad, I will not!" He hesitated for a moment, before he stated, "I am not allowed to! As this is your test not mine, and this journey you have endured could be the first of many. There! I've already said too much, ask no more questions."

"Alright, Uncle, let that be the last time, and from now on, I will endeavour to do my best, less selfishly. It does not mean that we cannot have a little fun together for the last time. Does it?"

"No, we can reminisce, and get to know each other for a short while. We shall never meet again if you complete your quest successfully," Ted blurted out.

"Why?" said Thomas.

"The simple answer is that you will not need me anymore!" laughed his beloved uncle.

A Strange Encounter

The exit lane from the railway station was paved with heavy cobble stones, and constructed to be durable, as it had withstood decades of heavy-duty wagons which had delivered coal which fed the ever-hungry steam trains and farm animals which were transported via rail and general traffic.

Many people found that when they walked upon those cobbles, they were quite tricky and precarious, but not for those two soldiers. Their heavy leather, laced-up military boots were sturdy and robust. Although, unlike Thomas's army boots, Ted's boots shone like sparkling, clean mirrors. Strangely, their boots were entirely impervious to the muck and grime upon the ground. Ted's overall image was that of an angel sent from Heaven, quite pristine and luminous; with a glowing aura which surrounded him!

As the two companions slowly marched down the lane, they encountered a well-dressed man, who gave the impression that he was of a certain age. His posture was very erect, and his manner very proper. Seemingly a vigilant man, who quickened his pace once he had noticed the two soldiers. The man had a large, Bullmastiff dog as his companion. Despite being grey around its muzzle, the dog was very muscular in appearance. The soldiers were surprised to see that the dog carried a small, black, leather briefcase, by holding the bag's leather handle within its mouth. The dog appeared to be friendly, as he approached the soldiers with a wagging tail and surprised them both when he sat down directly in front of them.

The Bullmastiff's master was several paces behind his dog, but as soon as his dog stopped, he sped up his pace in order to catch up with his companion. As the man moved closer to the soldiers, his eyes were blinded by bright sunlight. The man Gently rubbed his eyes, then stretched out his right hand and placed it on his forehead and he tried to block out that blinding sunbeam.

The soldiers stood motionless, as the dog sat pleadingly in front of them. The dog proceeded to smell their boots then inspected their uniforms. Once the dog was satisfied that the two soldiers were no threat to both him and his master, he sat down again, then raised a paw; his way of saying, 'Hello'.

It was at that precise moment that the dog's master too stood directly in front of the young, uniformed pals, and without hesitation said,

"Good morning, young men, you are a sight for sore eyes on this bright sunny day. Do you know, I could not believe my eyes when I saw my dog, Toby, offer his paw in friendship to you. He normally never leaves my side, and as for approaching strangers – well! You both must be the first! He is a good dog, amiable, so do not be afraid to pat him gently on his head and stroke him down his back. He is quite safe, so go on, show Toby that you are indeed friendly, as his paw is a sign of his friendship."

The two young men looked at this strange man and his dog in amazement. The dog's tail wagged so much, it acted like a yard-brush as it moved from side to side and swept away the dust that surrounded his rear-end.

Thomas was the first to lean forward and pat the dog gently on its head, and as its master laughed with glee. Ted too approached the big, friendly dog, knelt down on his right knee, and tickled the dog under its chin, then he stroked the dog's back, and said to the dog,

"There, there, Toby, you are a nice dog. Good boy."
Toby's master clapped his hands in glee and said to his dog,

"Yes, you are a good boy, and those villagers think you are too aloof! If only they could see you now, how proud I would be. Good boy, Toby."

At that same moment, the man patted his dog gently on its head, then offered his right hand, first, to one soldier, then the other and said,

"So, pleased to meet you both. What an unexpected pleasure for both Toby and me. Normally, I never have a chance to speak to anyone while approaching the station. I am always running late, you see, and in a terrible rush to catch the 9 am train."

Thomas and Ted nodded in answer to the man, but he had apparently not finished talking and continued,

"Toby, of course, does not get on the train with me, but carries my case onto Platform 1, then returns home. I live at the top of the hill, opposite a row of old cottages?"

The traveller looked up, noticed the two soldiers seemed amused but continued to explain himself,

"Please excuse an old man for his foolishness. Those cottages were knocked down years ago, and a small avenue of bungalows are there now – silly me. Well, nice meeting you, but before I continue my journey, may I ask why are you here lads, at this time of day? We don't see many soldiers around the village these days?"

Ted's reply was brief,

"We are both on a 'special pass' to see our family, due to an emergency."

Then, Thomas blurted out,

"My mum is ill, Sir. Maybe you know her? Her married surname is Williams, and my family used to live in one of those cottages at the top of the hill you mentioned. I think I remember you, sir. Are you Mr Wright, the local auctioneer?"

"Yes, I am, young man," he stood and stared at Thomas in bewilderment for a moment, then asked, "Are you Tommy Williams?" He shook his head, as if in disbelief!

Thomas softly answered,

"Afraid so, Mr Wright, and if you will excuse us both for being so abrupt in manner, we have an appointment to keep," Thomas looked at his uncle's ashen white face, then continued,

"Sir, you have a train to catch, we do not wish for you to miss it! Goodbye, sir." That man was transfixed to the spot on which he stood until his dog, Toby, nudged him with his cold, wet nose, barked loudly at him; as if to remind his master of their quest. The dog looked directly at the soldiers and made an almost inaudible whining noise, before he licked their hands affectionately. Toby placed his mouth on the handle of his master's case, lifted it off the ground, and continued his journey uphill towards the station's main entrance gate.

Meanwhile, Toby's master felt his body quiver as an ice-cold shiver ran down his spine. Seemingly, the old man felt uneasy in the presence of those two young soldiers, without the reassurance of his dog! The man turned on his heel and ran as fast as he could, to catch up with Toby. When he reached the turnstile gate, he instinctively turned around to wave goodbye, but to his astonishment, there was no sign of the soldiers.

While he fumbled with the latch upon the station gate, he mumbled,

"Surely, not! No, it could not have been Tommy Williams, he was killed while serving with our Paras, in Egypt! Then why would Toby stop to acknowledge them?" He shook his head, "I'll be glad to be on that platform where there are more people."

The two soldiers watched Mr Wright pass through the railway station's turn-style gate, as the 9am train entered the station, he took his briefcase from the dog's mouth, patted his dog on the head and gesticulated to the dog to return home.

As the dog, Toby, ran at full speed down the cobbled lane, he stopped momentarily in front of the two soldiers and jumped up to greet Thomas and Ted before he ran at full speed, up the hill towards his home.

That unexpected encounter left both pals' senses in a highly emotional state, and they exchanged puzzled expressions.

Thomas, unable to hold back any longer said,

"Did we just exchange greetings with two ghosts, mate? It was a bloody strange meeting. As for his dog, did you notice Toby vanished halfway up that hill!"

The soldiers stood momentarily frozen to the spot until once more Thomas shouted out,

"Look, the station has disappeared too!"

To which Ted replied,

"Timeless moments, mate, is to be expected to remind us both that it is time to move on."

Almost instantly, they continued to walk on towards the end of the lane, which adjoined the main road.

In contrast to the cobbled lane, the adjoining main road was tarmacked, and due to the sun having been at its highest point in the day, the air was warm, and the tarmac was soft under foot.

The two pals crossed that main road, which enabled them to use an ancient footpath.

It was a narrow footpath situated on the left-hand side of the main road and in grave disrepair. Over-hanging tree branches and hedges made walking perilous at the best of times, primarily because that pathway twisted and turned.

Their walking pace slowed, due to the onslaught of speeding cars oblivious to their safety. They decided it was safer to walk in 'single-file', so Ted took the lead.

As they slowly trudged onward up that ancient pathway, both men shared the same uncertainty, for they knew their reunion was to be short-lived but nevertheless essential, if they were to fulfil the essence of their quest.

The heat of the sun and the exertion of walking made both soldiers perspire profusely, as the sun's penetrating rays beat down upon their tired bodies, and they gazed at each other in amusement, due to their glowing pink faces.

Thomas could not contain himself any longer and spurted out,

"Blimey, I am out of condition, mate. I don't remember this bloody hill being so steep, the last time I was home."
Due to Thomas's outburst, both men slung their kitbags to the ground because their legs were weary. They decided to share Thomas's beaten-up, old leather, brown suitcase as their seat. They sat with their legs bent, as the traffic speeded by.

"Watch yourself, mate. We don't want our sodding legs chopped-off by those bloody cars, do we?" said Thomas's Uncle Ted, teasingly.

The soldier-pals mopped the sweat from their foreheads with their old khaki handkerchiefs. There they sat, as 'quiet as the grave', it gave them a moment to reflect on their present surroundings. A moment of respite when their senses enjoyed and observed nature at its best.

They delighted in hearing the high-pitched, melodious, song of a Blackbird that was sitting on a lowly branch above them. Their hearts filled with glee as they observed a Robin land upon the hedgerow behind them; busily eating wild blackberries, as if there were no tomorrow.

The soldiers shuffled backwards and tucked themselves tightly as possible into a hedge, because cars continued to pass them by, without a care for those resting soldiers.

Thomas broke their silent solitude when he asked,

"Have you ever heard a more delightful and beautiful sound, Ted, than the song of a Blackbird? I so missed the sounds of our British wild birds while in the Middle East – especially the early morning chorus. There is nothing to beat that, is there, mate?"

His companion nodded his head in agreement, and Thomas noticed a silent, lonely tear glide down his uncle's cheek, and instinctively gave his friend a gentle hug.

Thomas went on to state, "That is what I believe! The enchantment of being able to hear our feathered friends once more is quite spell-binding and priceless."

Ted was overwhelmed, he just smiled softly at his nephew then took out his handkerchief from his trouser pocket, wiped away the tears that trickled down his flushed cheeks and onto his jacket lapel.

The sharp barbs of the briars and thorny hedges scratched the soldiers as they squeezed tightly into them, but they did not bleed, when they instinctively tried to avoid those speeding cars.

That moment of rest enhanced the soldiers' awareness of the beauty which surrounded them both. They felt that the dense fauna and flora allowed them to watch and enjoy the antics of the wild birds without disturbing them.

They were overwhelmed by the scent of wild honeysuckle, primroses, bluebells, and apple blossom, which covered the embankments.

"Gosh, the perfume of the wild honeysuckle is quite lovely," declared Thomas.

Ted replied, "Nature allows a man to relax his very soul and enjoy the free gifts that it offers us all." The soldiers exchanged a knowing glance.

"Time is precious, so we cannot waste it. We must not dawdle any longer. Come, let us move forward, Thomas. Surely, you are excited to see your old home once again?"

"Just try stopping me, Uncle Ted! I'm ready to move if you are," said his excited nephew.

Both men rose from the ground and stretched their legs. Thomas wiped away red sand particles from his little case, threw his kitbag across his back and shouted, "Come on, pal, get a move on!"

Ted smirked at his pal, then he too quickly picked up his kitbag and sarcastically announced,

"Well, I'm ready to go, 'slow coach', what kept you!"

They both laughed out loud and walked in-step, till they found themselves at the top of that hill.

The Pauper's Cottages

The soldiers stood quite still at the top of the hill, Ted instinctively turned his body slightly to the right and gasped for breath. His eyes were transfixed upon an old, rusty iron railing separating the main road from an ancient cobbled lane, where a dejected old sign with weathered letters spelled out 'Paupers Cottages'.

"The cottages had been named after the poor tenants who lived there. Did you know that fact?" Ted asked Thomas.

"Yes! And look, that old sign is barely hanging on. Rust has eaten into its screws where it contacted the fencing," replied Thomas.

Ted was filled with joy when he saw the sign and said,

"Look, Thomas! Can you believe it, the old sign is still there after all this time?"

But the time it took Thomas to turn his head, to the right, was too slow. Ted gasped because his eyes seemed to have played tricks on him.

"What the hell!" he exclaimed.

The scene had changed, the reality of that situation, was that a cul-de-sac of modern bungalows, with neatly manicured lawns had replaced their old homes. Cars, like they had never seen before, were parked in front of each driveway.

Ted turned and faced his nephew, and said, "I tell you now Thomas, my eyes must have played tricks on me. I swore only a moment ago, our old cottages were there right in front of us, but now, they are gone."

"I saw them, Uncle Ted – just for a second or two," replied Thomas.

"Then, where have they gone, mate?" retorted Ted.

Both men stood and gazed at the modern bungalows, which had replaced their old home, puzzled and in utter shock and dismay.

Thomas and his uncle allowed their minds to slip gently back in time, to when they were children, and the scene once more changed before their eyes, and their old cottages stood before them once more.

A row of six ancient, run-down, white-washed brick cottages appeared before them, and children played games outside. The children shouted at a large convoy of USA lorries, filled with American Airmen from the nearby airfield. The airmen were busy throwing oranges and small bars of chocolate to the children. While several young girls clapped their hands with joy, the young boys scurried to pick up the free treats which had landed on the ground. The young boys filled their trouser pockets, then threw the excess gifts to the toddlers and girls, who tried their best to catch the goodies with open arms.

The children cried out to the airmen for more sweets,

"Hey, Yanks, have you got any more chocolate bars? My mum loves chocolate."

The American soldier who wore several stripes upon the shoulder of his uniform, laughed loudly, then said,

"Catch this, kid… Have you never seen an orange before…? Where is your older sister then?"

Both Ted and Thomas enjoyed that shared visual memory and laughed at having seen children's joyful antics. They instinctively knew that they were watching Thomas and his friends in another time and place!

Not all their shared memories were happy or pleasant ones, they had experienced the constant tummy pains derived from hunger.

Living in overcrowded, tumble-down cottages, that had walls riddled with cockroaches, meant they were prone to illness and childhood diseases. Too often, such unsanitary living conditions led to early deaths or disabilities and Diphtheria and Polio epidemics were a constant threat to such a poor community.

Suddenly, the reality of their childhood overcame Thomas and he cried out,

"We never really knew where the next meal was coming from in those days, did we, Ted?"

Nevertheless, they knew that they had survived such a difficult childhood, so grinned at each other and decided to recall their good memories. Their shared experience had been delightful and when they saw those yellow balls tossed into the air by those airmen, Thomas said,

"They called them oranges, I remember that I asked, "What's an orange, mister? They all burst out laughing at my ignorance and shouted at us kids," 'Oranges are an exotic fruit, dummies.'

Ted was amused and shook his head, and gave his pal a teasing look as Thomas continued his story,

"Like, we bloody cared where that yellow ball came from, or what it was called, eh? We just wanted to know if we could eat the bloody thing. When I sunk my teeth into that first orange, my teeth froze. Its bitterness stung my tongue and throat. I recollect my tongue went a bright yellow colour and hurt for days after eating so many of those oranges."

The soldier remembered the American airmen's reactions, after the children had tasted an exotic fruit for the first time.

"The Airmen were in fits of laughter and shouted to us, 'You have to peel the fruit first, dummies! Peel off the outer skin. You kids have eaten the peel, don't you know how to eat an orange? Firstly, you break it into segments. Go on, dummies, try it, and you will love the sweet taste, go on, do it!'"

Ted and Thomas smiled as in their mind's eye, they watched those children peel the oranges with their grubby little fingers, split them into quarters, then divided them carefully between their gang members. The eldest lad blurted out to the watching airmen,

"You are right, mates, 'tis good, sweet and juicy – any more exotic fruits going spare, mates?"

The soldiers watched those children wave their new Yank friends goodbye as they departed in their military trucks.

They also observed how that group of children worked as a team when they collected the rest of the oranges that had been strewn across the pathway and main road.

It amused the soldiers to see that the children were careful when they placed the oranges into their old coat pockets. Several lads took off their jackets and used them to carry the excess oranges and chocolate bars. Girls lifted up their skirts and petticoats to hold their share of the exotic fruit and sweets.

The most prominent lad in the group took charge of all the goodies collected and divided them between the relevant families – based upon how many there were in each individual family. Those children came from underprivileged families, and so everyone looked out for their friends.

Thomas started to reminisce, "I remember, our mum's homemade jam was sweetened with local honey, as there was no sugar in the shops during wartime. Our convoys were not allowed to carry imported goods, such as sugar, so people improvised by using honey and carrots to sweeten their foods. God! It was a welcome treat to our poor diets."

"Marmalade, it was called marmalade," teased Ted.

"Yes, it was, and we were fed marmalade 'hot toddies', instead of expensive medicine, when children went down with diphtheria. I remember sleeping well after Dad put a little Navy Rum into our night drinks," continued Thomas.

Ted shared one of his memories, "The community spirit was excellent, especially amongst the more impoverished sector of our village. It was quite common to 'borrow' or 'lend' a bowl of porridge oats, tea, flour, and other essential commodities.

Families were often made up of large numbers of children in those days, as 'family planning' was unheard of. Underprivileged families always seemed to live in the smallest cottages – usually 'two up and two down'! Such families were always short of space, so several children had to share beds, sleeping 'head-to-toe'."

Suddenly, Thomas decided to share another childhood memory with his uncle, "Do you remember how it was at bedtime, Ted? How our parents used to shout at us all from downstairs," he paused for a moment, then continued. 'Girls at one end of the large bed and boys at the other end, no messing now. Get to sleep.' "We were all sent to bed after a cold supper which consisted of dry bread and homemade dripping, with salt and pepper on top. If it was a cold night, Dad spread mustard pickle over our butties, and called it a 'hot meal' for God's sake!"

Both soldiers broke out in laughter.

Thomas continued,

"It was quite a scramble, as we children fought to get the best position in that one, large, wooden bed. It seemed a huge bed at that time, with so many old mattresses placed one on top of the other. The iron springs below the mattresses were so old, many poked through, and prodded us when we turned over during the night. But it never seemed to bother us, as we took it for granted that that was how everyone slept in their beds."

Ted laughed and chuckled with his pal at the very thought of seven kids fighting with feather-filled pillows, till they finally fell asleep exhausted.

Thomas went on to tell his pal how "It was during those winter nights that Dad used to throw his old WWI heavy, khaki woollen 'great-coat' on the top of our bed; to keep us from freezing in our bed. Do you remember that bloody old coat, Uncle Ted?" he asked.

Ted stayed silent and waited for his nephew to continue.

"The great-coat was double lapelled, and still had the original brass buttons down the front. During the colder months, dad wore it to work. We were taught, not to throw or waste good clothing in those days. We were too sodding poor to be over-proud."

Ted nodded in agreement.

Thomas explained, "As we lay there under the weight of those bloody blankets and that stinky old greatcoat, we all snuggled up to each other to try to keep warm. The older ones told ghost stories to their younger siblings. Our Johnny being the youngest of us, was so frit, he hid under the covers. Johnny only popped his bloody head up to watch the twinkling stars that shone upon us through that rotting old tiled roof. The rain dripped through the old tiles onto the floor – sometimes onto us. Seemed to us that Dad was forever emptying those old white, enamel buckets during stormy winter nights. He'd placed enamel buckets at strategic points around our room to catch the rain and the buckets of rainwater were then emptied into an old tin bath; as we never wasted good water. Bloody hell, mate, they called those days 'the good old days', didn't they!"

Ted finally spoke, "Yes, our families were poverty-stricken, which left us all no choice, but to be fugal and never take our dire situation for granted.

We inhabitants were just grateful to enjoy the luxury of having a 'roof over our heads'. Few villagers owned their own homes so, lived in rented accommodation under the ever watchful eyes of unscrupulous landlords. The land where tenanted dwellings were situated, were worth more than the cottages that stood upon it. The welfare of the sickly 'renters' was of no concern to greedy landlords."

Thomas nodded his head.

"We never knew what it was to wear new clothes, enjoy new toys for Christmas or birthdays or sit down to a full roast dinner on Sunday. Most families lived on a pan of rabbit stew. It was tasty though and filling. We dunked dry bread into the gravy, and no one ever left anything on their plates in those days."

Ted asked his nephew, "I guess that you too left school with only a fundamental education at fourteen years of age?"

Thomas replied, "Sure did! My first job was as a farm labourer, then I moved on to work in a coal yard, where I was taught to drive vehicles; I stayed in that position until 'called up' to 'fight for King and Country'. The armed forces allowed us both – at different periods of time of course; to improve ourselves. Military pay was a lot better than our lowly farm wages, no doubt about that."

Thomas pondered for a moment, then, "Fifteen bloody shillings a week wasn't much to live on, was it, mate? Being a soldier seemed a lot better than all that sweat for nowt. Once we gave Dad our 'board and lodging money', there was little left for ourselves, eh, mate? Nevertheless, the big lad's wages were a necessary input to our family's income! Dad was classed as 'casual labour' which meant he could be 'laid off' work anytime without warning, so, he got a higher rate on the farms than regular employees. He had to be able to 'turn his hands' to any work available, as his farm work was seasonal. Guess he did his best, as times were hard back in those days!"

Thomas's mind was still in the past as he bellowed out,

"Hand-me-downs, remember, Uncle Ted, that's all we ever knew while growing up. Other peoples' sodding 'cast-offs', which meant that Mum and Granny spent many evenings unpicking seams, cutting out patterns, sewing for hours on end; with only candlelight to see, just so we had clothes to cover our backsides."

Ted, looked at his nephew and smiled,

"Too bloody true! I grew up in those cottages too, mate, well before you, so you cannot tell me how it was. I never had a suit to my name till I joined the Royal Marines, and that day was the proudest day of my life."

Ted's voice lowered to a whisper, as sorrowful tears slowly trickled down his cheeks, as he explained,

"Seemed to me, lad, we never knew what it was to live like proper human beings until we joined the forces, what do you say, Thomas lad?"

Thomas dropped his head in shame and empathised with his beloved uncle, and just nodded his head while he wiped away tears that flowed profusely from his eyes.

"Let's think of happier times while we walk on, lad, it does not pay to dwell too much on the past, for we cannot change it."

Thomas, wore a frown on his face, when he noticed his uncle Ted's eyes had filled up with tears of regret, and yet, that frown turned into a beaming smile after he blurted out,

"Forever the optimist, Uncle Ted, eh?" It was at that moment Thomas realised they had just shared their childhood memories, despite being born a generation apart, which in turn had strengthened the bond between them.

Ted paused then asked Thomas,

"Haven't you got any funny, happier memories that you can share with me?"

Thomas turned to look directly at his uncle, and said, "As a matter of fact, I have, so listen up, here comes a funny story!

Jerry Under the Bed

Ted patted his nephew gently upon his right shoulder and laughed, and asked him,

"Do you remember the night your dad introduced you to the 'Jerry', Thomas?"

Thomas turned to meet his uncle's eyes and burst out into a hysterical laughter, and replied,

"Damn right, I bloody do, mate, for we all fell for that one. Shall I tell you what happened that freezing cold night? Well, listen up!

"All us kids were sent to bed for our kip early as the village siren went off. It happened as we were all halfway through our supper so, we were all bloody scared. We took our dripping butties to bed with us and snuggled up under the blankets for comfort. No one was a 'scared cat'! No one shouted out for Mum or cried, we just huddled together and ate our butties, as brave soldiers do.

"Until suddenly, our kid, Roly, shouted out,

"'I need the lavvy, Mum, needs to do number two, needs to do it now; just cannot wait. Mum, Dad, where are you?'

"Then the door opened at the bottom of the stairs, and Dad's head appeared at the top of the stairs – opposite our bed. He looked at us all huddled together under the blankets, then at our brother, Roly, who was still moaning for the lavvy, and whispered quietly,

"'The Jerry's under the bed, kids!'"

Thomas continued his story,

"Before, you could say 'Jack Robinson'! All hell broke loose as we shot out of that bloody bed, like bullets out of a gun. We pushed past Dad so fast and hard, we near knocked him off his sodding feet and we all charged downstairs. Once we hit the bottom tread, we all hid under the sodding stair hole. Every one of us trembled, because we were so frightened. Honestly, Ted, we thought Hitler himself was after us, and we stayed hidden under the old stair hole.

"Bloody hell mate! Some of us had wet ourselves with fright, and as for our Roly, well, his pants were full of shite before he hit the bottom of the sodding stairs.

"So, there, our brother, Roly, sat all huddled up, with his knees brought upright under his chin and stinking to high Heaven, while sobbing. He was so frit; in case he was given a bloody hiding for messing his pants. All we could do was laugh, and I still remember the lingering stink of sweat and fear; from when we were all huddled together under those bloody stairs, mate – even to this day!

"Anyway, my mum and dad appeared in front of us kids and near laughed their bloody heads off, so much so, my mum's face was all flushed and red like. She stared directly at our kid, Roly, smiled all sweet-like at him, then she looked back at Dad and they both laughed at us until I cried out,

"'What's so funny?'

"'You all are,' replied Dad.

"Then our mum said softly to us all, 'Come on out of there, you are all a silly lot. Didn't you know the chamberpot was nicknamed 'Jerry' when War II broke out!'

"She dragged us out from under those wooden stairs, one-by-one, as none of us wanted to leave that safe hidey hole.

"So, yes! I sure do remember the first time my dad introduced us all to the 'Jerry', Uncle Ted! Tell you what, bets on our Roly remembers it too."

Both men laughed so loud that neither of them looked the other in the eye but turned their heads in different directions to tried to regain their composure.

Eventually, Thomas let out a big grumpy sigh as he bellowed out to his Uncle Ted,

"Yes, we poor kids had it rough in the bloody war, mate, and due to all the bombing raids in London, Liverpool and other major cities, our small village – like many other places

– took in dozens of townie kids that had been evacuated into the countryside.

We felt sorry for those evacuated kids – as poor as we were. They were sent away, far from home with nowt but their gas masks, the clothes they stood up in, and a small bag holding their few treasures such as a teddy bear. Many kids did not even have a photo of their mum and dad to give them reassurance, so everyone in our village pitched in to give them a few old clothes, made them welcome and many of our village kids shared their beds with them as well."

Ted nodded in agreement.

His nephew grumbled, "Bet the bloody nob's kids never went to bed hungry because of bloody rationing. Oh, no! It has always been the same, one bloody rule for the rich, and another for the poor, mate. So, bollocks to those top nobs, I say!"

Ted was shocked by his nephew's outburst and disgruntled manner but allowed him to let off steam.

Thomas asked his Uncle Ted, "Do you remember enjoying thick rounds of locally baked bread, still hot from the local bakery here? Our mum used to send us kids down to the village bakery each morning to buy our family's daily ration of Penny buns.

"Sometimes, we used to pinch out small pieces of the hot crust, from the underside of those loaves, because we were so hungry. Mum must have known, yet she never complained. Such good old days, mate!"

Ted nodded his head.

"Always cheaper when the bread was a day old, remember that?" remarked Thomas as he continued to reminisce.

"Stale or not! Bread was the 'Staff of Life' for us undernourished kids, as we were always hungry, and suppertime was the highlight of our day. I daresay, you remember how our tummies grumbled during the night.

"Remember how our mums used to place Grandma's old China meat plate in the middle of the table, stacked high with thickly cut rounds of stale bread, spread thickly with dollops of dripping. Sometimes, she placed pickles on top. My favourite topping was her homemade carrot or bramble jelly.

I loved the bramble jelly best, primarily as we children had contributed to the bounty because we had collected pounds of berries from the hedgerows in nearby fields.

"I recall it took us all hours to fill our mum's old wicker basket with wild blackberries – just so our mum could make bramble jelly. Mum also used her blackberry jelly for medicinal purposes in the wintertime, especially during an influenza epidemic. She placed a teaspoon of blackberry jelly into a cup, poured on boiling water and called it blackberry tea. We also used to collect wild Rosehips which mum made a syrup from, which was used for medicinal purposes only. Delicious, Ted."

Both men licked their lips and their mouths watered with delight at the thought of such a childhood treat.

Ted intervened, "It is nice to chat about the old days, especially as we never had the chance to know each other as children. All information about you kids came from letters sent to me by your dad, but letters from home always arrived months after being sent. I did manage to send a few photos back home, one of which showed us Navy lads celebrating the crossing of the Equator. Our battle cruiser, *The Exeter*, visited Chile and I purchased a postcard and sent it to my brother – whether he received it or not – I've no idea! Strange, that I only remember the beginning of the battle in the river plate, but not the end."

He paused momentarily to say, "Or, should I say, my end!"

His nephew found it difficult to swallow as the intensity of Ted's shared memory troubled them both. As it was obvious that he found their paradoxical union confusing, as he wiped those sad tears from his eyes. Not wanting his pal to dig deeper into that memory, despite his empathy with his uncle's quandary, he answered his friend,

"I remember seeing a photograph of you and your mates, fooling about by jumping into the sea, cos dad showed it to us all.

Dad was so proud when you crossed the Equator whilst serving on The Exeter, because none of our family had ever travelled abroad before; except Granny's relatives, who had emigrated to Canada.

He also said that you are a hero and we must never forget you, and I never did. Uncle Ted, you are my hero, or why would you be here with me now?"

Ted smiled sweetly at Thomas when he answered,

"I see your point; it is always best to dwell on the happy times in our lives." The marine sighed, then continued to say, "Do you remember anything else about those Yanks, mate?"

Playing Soldiers and
Making New Friends

Thomas continued with a smirk on his face,

"I remember that having those Yanks around certainly livened up our community and most of us kids were excited when we saw them arrive in their big trucks.

One day, while our gang of lads sat on a hill which overlooked our home, bored stiff, until we spotted one of the Yank's vehicles enter a local farmer's field pulling an enormous anti-aircraft gun. We ran like bats outa hell to get a closer look and check what they were up to.

"The farmer saw us and shouted at us, 'Sod off home, you little brats. This business is nowt' to do with you!'"

Thomas laughed at his own story, then continued,

"Lads being lads, full of mischief, we pretended to leave the area then circled around that field. We scrambled under the wire fencing and came up from the riverside of the field. When we all lifted our heads up from the riverbank, the Yanks spotted us, burst out laughing, then gesticulated at us and we took that as an invitation to join them. They said they were there to set up a giant anti-aircraft gun on top of the hill to protect the village from German bombers.

"We could not believe our luck to be there when they unlocked that gun from its hook on the back of their truck. The gun had wheels attached to it, which allowed the Yanks to swivel it around. When those Yanks pulled and pushed that gun up a hill, they sweated and cursed – after all, it was a sweltering afternoon. The field was muddy from a storm from the previous night, so the steeper their climb became, the more those Yanks slithered about. Believe me, Ted, we sat there on our backsides and giggled because of the new swear words we heard."

The thought of his nephew having heard American slang for the first time made Ted roll about with fits of laughter.

His nephew laughed, as he explained his youngest brother Roly's high pitched voice shout out,

"'They said, FUCK! What does that mean, Tommy? Now they keep shouting 'Shit'! Do they need to go to the lavvy? I'm sure our mum would let them use ours.'

"The Yanks heard our brother's outburst and roared with laughter which sent him into such a temper so, he stuck his tongue out at them. We thought he would end up with a clipped ear, but no!

The American soldier in charge of his group shouted," 'Hey kids, how'd you like to have a go on our gun, then?'

"Bloody hell, Ted, we didn't need a second invitation, but ran up that hill like bats outa hell, sat on the ground next to them with eyes like saucers. We sat as quiet as mice as we watched them align the gun as they told us that the gun needed to face the village. It was better than reading our adventure comics – a real adventure; especially when one of the Yanks asked us,

"'Do you want to take turns to sit on the seat while we align the gun? Maybe if you are quiet, we will let you have had a go at shooting those German bombers down.'

"'Yes, mister, we'd love to have a go,' cried out our Roly in his excited high voice.

"We took turns as we played around with that anti-aircraft gun and in our imaginative minds, we shot down more bombers than we could count, and a Yank shouted at us,' So, kids you enjoy playing soldiers.'

"They stank of foreign tobacco, but I was fascinated by the fact that they seemed to have an endless supply of commercial cigarettes; whereas dad stored his rationed tobacco in an old, sweet tin.

Suddenly, one of the Yanks shouted to me," 'Fancy a cigarette, young man? Do you smoke? Are you allowed to smoke cigarettes at your age then?'

"I replied in my best grown up voice, 'Yes, of course we do, how about giving us a few ciggies then.'

"Then a tall, dark-haired soldier took out a new packet of cigarettes from his uniform's top pocket and gave each one of us a readymade cigarette. His mate retrieved a silver military-style lighter from his jacket pocket, flicked it, until a flame appeared, and one by one lit them for us – even our Roly had one.

The Yanks stood silent with smirks on their faces and watched us take a deep draw from those ciggies, until our Roly's cheeks started to go pale, then pink, then a greenish colour; just before he threw up, right on top of that Yank's clean and shiny boots.

The Yanks seemed to have found the whole affair funny except the poor sod, who ended up with our Roly's breakfast all over his bloody shiny boots! That miserable sod snatched the ciggies' out of our gobs and that disgruntled Yank threw them on the ground as his temper exploded.

One of his mates, who had a croaky voice, most likely from smoking too much, thrust his hands up into the air and said, 'What did you expect, you idiot! Giving kids of their age cigarettes, they are too young to smoke!'

"He then turned to me, and asked politely, 'Tell me, have you ever smoked a cigarette before, kid?'

I replied, "Of course I have, mister. I pinch my dad's tobacco when he is asleep, as all us big lads do; then we smoke our homemade ciggies together, in our gang's secret den.'

After a moments' silence, that Yank looked me straight in the eye and everyone seemed to get the joke, as they burst out into laughter. The Yank, whose boots our kid had spewed up on, had finished cleaning off the sick with a spare canister of water that was attached to his belt. He looked up at me when and said, 'You're a cheeky little devil for sure, I'll give you that, and for your cheek, you can keep the rest of that packet of cigarettes. Take them home and give them to your dad, with my compliments, but don't tell him I gave cigarettes to kids, okay!'

"I grabbed that packet of cigarettes before he changed his mind, then slipped them into my back trouser pocket. We spent the rest of the afternoon with those Yanks, they were great fun.

By teatime, their senior officer turned up in a big jeep and they told us to 'Go home, lads, it is time for you to make yourselves disappear, or you'll get us all into trouble. Go back home, the way you came, so our officer cannot see you. Okay, go quickly now, move yourselves!'

"We all saluted our new friends and they all saluted us back in their Yankee way, and I winked and gave them a thumbs up to say, 'thank you'. They stood to attention and saluted us, because I think, they too enjoyed our company as much as we enjoyed theirs.

As we prepared ourselves to leave, they chatted amongst themselves, until one Yank laughed out loud after being nudged by his mate who then shouted, " 'Don't forget to give our regards to your big sisters, we Yanks are a friendly lot, okay!'

"Our little kid, Roly, spurted out, 'What does that Yank mean, Thomas? We have not got any big sisters.'
"The big lads giggled, for most of the way home but our kid just looked puzzled and went into one of his sulks'.

After our supper that night, we were so tired from our daytime adventures, we climbed those wooden hills willingly. Not much sleep was had by us, except our Roly, who was out like a light turned off – as soon as his head hit the pillow. The rest of us giggled and whispered as we passed on our day's adventures to our three sisters."

Ted enquired, "Did you give your dad that packet of cigarettes, Thomas?"

"Like hell, we did, we hid them under our pillow and the next day, added them to our gang's stash, in our old wooden treasure box marked 'Secret' on the top of its lid. Do you know, Ted that we never opened that packet of cigarettes, as they were proof of our day's adventure, being foreign ciggies and all! Anyway, my dad used to say he preferred his Woodbines to foreign tobacco, so guess we did him a favour!"

"Did you see any other foreigners in our village during the war, Thomas?"

"Yes, there were a few POWs and Italians towards the end of the war, and most of them worked on the local farms, along with the land girls, and quite a lot of them married local girls and settled down in the village.

"Any more stories you want to share with me, Thomas?' said Ted.

Thomas nodded his head, "I remember too seeing a large army troop carrier, filled with allied Czechoslovakian soldiers, that had parked outside the local pub that adjoins the Canal towpath. We village kids stood transfixed as that group of foreign soldiers jumped out of the troop carrier one by one and started to set up a soup kitchen.

"I remember how the smell of fresh meat and vegetables in that cooking pot made my nostrils twitch with excitement and my tummy rumbled with anticipation; we kids were always hungry back then. Anyway, we watched that saucepan until our mouths began to water and wondered what they intended to do with all that food. The local pub landlord kept sending out jugs of ale for the soldiers, and locals began to gather around that mobile kitchen. As the crowd grew in numbers, everyone there chatted, shook hands, and generally made friends with the visitors.

Suddenly, the soldiers announced to the crowd of onlookers,"

'Please, come and taste our good soup, we welcome you, as you have welcomed us – not as strangers, but as friends.'

"Believe me, Uncle Ted, no one was shy at coming forward that afternoon, as people gathered around to enjoy a bowl of their tasty, hot soup washed down with a flagon of free ale, and a kind of spontaneous party broke out. I tell you this, we all left for home with full bellies and happily sang all the way home.

My mum, like many villagers, missed that free meal, because a local farmer arrived in the village square at 8am that morning in his tractor, which was pulling a low-loader trailer. It was the beginning of the potato picking season for farmers and local labour was cheap and available. The only way to get to the local farms outside the village was by everyone to sit tightly together on that bloody old trailer. Those hard boards made one's bottom sore so, the women took a soft cushion, to sit on."

Ted, interrupted his nephew to say, "I remember 'Potato Picking week'

Thomas smiled, then continued relaying his story, "Yes, it was just the same for us all, as schools closed for a whole week, which enabled villagers to work on the farms at peak times. It was a chance for underprivileged families to earn extra cash. Guess we all helped the government's economy grow, as even children were allocated a strip of land, next to their mothers, to pick potatoes.

"I remember earning a few shillings by the end of the working week, and the farmers needed our labour. Farmers generally allowed us a lot of freedom to play around the farm buildings, fed us at lunchtime, which meant that no one returned home till twilight.

"Usually, we went with our mum to help her pick spuds all day, as the more sacks of potatoes we filled from our allocated lot in the field, the more money we earned as a family. Our kid, Roly, had been up all night being sick, so we were told to stay at home, in case it turned out to be anything infectious.

"The only thing we caught was a free hot meal of soup, served with warm, jacket potatoes, which the soldiers had cooked on an open fire. We were delighted in watching them place a nob of fresh, farm butter inside each jacket potato and they served each meal on old military tin plates. Believe me, Uncle Ted, that night must have been the only night I can remember, that we all went to bed on a full stomach – such a happy feeling!"

Ted looked at his nephew's face, that glowed with excitement from having shared his childhood memories. Ted smiled, patted Thomas on the back, and declared,

"Well, I certainly never thought that while serving in the Navy, my young nephew and his merry gang of friends back home were enjoying such a jolly war, by experiencing a once in a lifetime adventure and making so many new friends too. Blimey! Your exploits make my experiences at sea look quite insignificant."

"They are just a young lad's childhood memories, Uncle Ted." He paused for a moment, then said, "What is life all about if we cannot remember the good times, share our joys and sorrows with a friend? All I can remember thinking to myself, while in Egypt, was that whatever happened while I was so far from home, I would return home one day and no one, nor anything, could stop me from fulfilling that quest."

Ted decided to change the subject, so asked, "What was my beloved brother up to, while I was away in the Navy? I know he never missed a chance to have a game of cards and he hardly ever lost his stake money when he and the local men played 'Crown and Anchor'. He always nominated himself as the Banker in charge of the game itself, which allowed him to control the game and as such, he hardly ever lost any money."

Ted remembered,

"Your dad always insisted on being the Banker as it suited his purpose, and that was to gain every penny out of amateur players. It may have been classed as an illegal game but that never stopped the men of the village playing it at home, or after hours as a 'private party' in the local pubs."

"Let me think back, Uncle Ted, for I do remember one incident when Yanks were stationed nearby our village," replied Thomas.

Thomas knew he had his uncle's attention because Ted idolised his big brother, who was his beloved dad. Thomas knew his own dad thought the world of Ted as he was his youngest brother. Thomas's dad was especially proud of his youngest brother because he had joined the Royal Marines and trained as a gunner on one of our prestigious battle ships.

Both men lit themselves another cigarette, took deep breaths and deeply inhaled the tobacco; before Thomas started to tell his uncle another 'tell-tale' story.

"You have to realise, mate, that my dad never knew we kids used to follow him and the other local men. We always kept our ears to the ground – especially if we got a drift of something fishy, or should I say, illegal was about to happen."

Thomas explained, "Well! One Saturday morning, we boys were sitting on the stairs listening to our parents' conversation at the breakfast table. We often sat on those wooden stairs to listen to the grownups talking, as they never allowed us to read newspapers or explained grownup stuff.

"Hearing our dad ask, 'I need a packed lunch, Mother, as I will be out all day but hopefully, I will return home in time for supper a little richer. Don't forget to make a flask of raw tea as I dislike Bovril, and Camp Coffee as it is just too sweet for my taste.'

"I once asked my dad a question, using the word 'why', and he looked me in the eye, before he fobbed me off, when he said, 'Why is a crooked letter and you cannot straighten it. Ask no questions, then you'll receive no lies.'

"So, we quickly learnt to keep our gobs shut, ask no questions, keep our ears and eyes open; as one learns a lot more truth that way. Anyway, there we sat, all huddled together on the bottom step, as quiet as mice, listening through the cracks of the closed door.

"As soon as Dad left the house, Mum went to the scullery to do some washing, so we spied our chance to follow Dad.

"We sneakily hid behind the outside lavvy wall to see where Dad was going carrying a sizeable shoulder bag, which Mum had made for him out of a potato sack. This bag was used by Dad to carry his working week's packed lunches, along with a few work tools; but it was a Saturday, so we knew he was up to mischief!

"'He doesn't work on Saturdays, so where is he off to?' asked our kid, Roly, as he never had learnt Dad's rule, 'do not ask questions'.

"Give our Roly due credit, Ted, he was right on that score, so we then knew something fishy was definitely about to happen. We discreetly followed Dad into the village and as he walked over the Canal Bridge, we quickly slid down the canal batter and hid under the bridge itself.

"The Canal bridge was adjacent to the Queen's Arms Public House and was a perfect place for us kids to hide under. We did not have to wait long before several of Dad's old mates joined him. Shortly afterwards, an army lorry arrived, and several Yanks jumped out of the vehicle. After a lot of whispering and shaking hands, Dad and his mates climbed into the truck along with the Yanks and the vehicle sped off towards the outskirts of the village."

"You were outmanoeuvred then, lad," mocked Ted.

"No way, mate! Roly, being so small, had climbed on his hands and knees through the bramble bushes that grew alongside the canal batter. There, he hid quietly, listening to the grownups' conversations.

"He heard one of Dad's mate whisper, 'Right! lads, let' make our way to Blue Bell Woods to enjoy a few games of 'Crown and Anchor' with our Yankee friends. This time we can play for real money and hopefully, empty our visiting friends' pockets.'

"Dad and his mates burst into laughter, much to the curiosity of the Yanks, who were not within hearing distance.

"Once we knew where they were all going, we headed back home as we knew a shortcut to Blue Bell Woods. We knew we could get there before the grownups, and we did. Our early arrival gave us time to climb up a giant oak tree which was in full leaf at that time, a perfect place to hide unseen. It was an excellent spot to pick, as it overlooked the clearing in the wood; where our dad had held his card parties before. We had a den hidden nearby in the bushes to conceal ourselves, if the military police or the local cop got wind of this illegal gathering.

"It took us about ten minutes to settle ourselves into a giant hole halfway up that old oak tree and it was a bit of a squeeze, despite having left our Roly back at the den site, cos he couldn't keep quiet for long.

We sat all crunched up together in that hole in the tree for at least an hour, when Dad suggested, real casual like, that they introduce the Yanks to the game of 'Crown and Anchor'. 'Does any of you Yanks got any English money in those wallets of yours?' asked Dad.

"The Yanks talked amongst themselves for a few minutes, checked their wallets, then a bloke with stripes on his shoulder, piped up, 'Yeah, plenty of British coins and quite a bit of paper money, so hope you guys can match our money pot.'

"The Yanks proceeded to empty their wallets into their caps and place their caps directly in front of them. Dad and his mate's eyes nearly popped out as handfuls of small silver, half-Crowns, ten bob notes and a heap of copper change emerged. Believe me, Dad's face lit up like a firework on bonfire night. Confident that he would return home with his pockets full of 'easy money'.

"Well, Ted, a lot of cursing, fist banging took place on that makeshift, gambling table as Dad did his magic! Nevertheless, just at dusk, we heard a lot of commotion coming from the far field. The eldest lad climbed up to the top of the oak tree to get a better view of the strangers approaching, and suddenly shouted out, 'Look out, everyone, several Yanks are approaching and they have red caps on their heads. Now, they are running towards our wood.'

"We shouted down to the men, who were startled to hear kids' voices coming from above them, 'Dad, the Yankee MPs, are coming, you had better run quick! Quickly, they will be here in a minute.'

"The Yanks were the first to 'up and run' as they knew they'd end up in jail if they got caught red-handed taking part in an illegal gambling game.

"Then our dad looked up at our tree, waved and shouted out, 'You are good lads! Looking after your old dad, see you all at home.'

"Dad quickly picked up the 'Crown and Anchor' cloth, placing the dice carefully into his small metal dice tin. Believe me, he did not forget to pick up the money left on the ground and placed them all into his dinner-bag. Dad was a canny bloke and proved it by telling his mates to run in opposite directions to confuse the MPs; that way they all managed to get home safely due to the confusion.

"By the time those Yankee MPs arrived, there was nobody around to arrest and we hid in our underground den until we were damn sure they had all left the area.

Our kid, Roly, had fallen asleep on a pile of leaves while all this was going on and when we told him what had happened, he said, 'Cor, what a great story, just like listening to 'Dick Barton, Special Agent' on the Wireless. Promise, you'll tell me more tonight, while we're in bed, cos the girls will only believe it if you tell the story.'

"We were all so excited, until a mate of mine suggested, 'How about we go check out that place again, to see if they left anything behind.'

"Hey, Ted, have you ever felt that frightened that you feared you'd mess your pants? Every leaf on those ghostly oak trees seemed to rustle, watching our every move.

Nevertheless, our quest payed off as we filled our pockets with coins of every description and Roly found a fiver on the trail leading out of the wood. Must have been a Yank's fiver, as no villager would be wealthy enough to carry that much money unless they were Black Marketers and my dad was not one of them, nor were his mates; but he was nicknamed, 'The Banker', get it? Bank – Banker."

At that last outburst, both companions laughed, until their stomach's hurt so much, they loosened their belts slightly to breathe and both agreed it was a great story.

Ted said, "Well, young man, you certainly managed to impress someone upstairs, for here you are! Now, what are we to do with this Heavenly gift? It is time to come to terms with the present and happily continue seeking out those who are an important part of this difficult quest!"

Family Life

The soldiers stood at the top of the hill, memories of their childhood days lingered and the illusion of those old cottages had become an imprinted image in their minds, which had suddenly transpired from a strange mist – right before their eyes.

It was at this this point that both men looked directly at each other and smiled, as to experience the irony of their memory which conflicted with reality. Solemn cottages stood before them, and they gazed at the homes which gradually became visible and stood directly in front of them.

"Just look at them, Uncle Ted, typical 'Jerry-built' cottages, rotten from the foundations to the roof. One had to be from the lower classes to have lived in such places and no matter how hard we all worked, life was rough," cried out Thomas.

"Then say 'Goodbye' to your old home now, for you will never have to see it again, Thomas," replied Ted.

Thomas's anger spilled out, "Dad used to say, 'A poor man sheds blood, sweat and tears to earn the top rate in agriculture, even then it is never enough money to make ends meet.' He was so bloody right, cos no matter how hard we all pulled together, life was tough, and times never seemed to get any easier in those days."

Ted was jolted by his nephew's return to self-pity and replied,

"Come on, lad, buck up! Let us think of happier times while we walk on. It does no good to dwell too much on sad memories. We cannot change the past."

Thomas's scowl turned into a smirk, when he lifted his face upwards to observe his uncle's facial expression and checked whether those former teary eyes had dried but was surprised when he perceived a sparkle of amusement there,

"Forever the optimist, eh, Uncle Ted?" he replied.

The realisation that they had shared their childhood memories had given Thomas comfort, especially as they were born over a generation apart. Something he had never, in his wildest dreams, could have anticipated was the chance to be with his childhood hero.

Thomas spoke out, "We were just so impoverished, yet thankful, to have a roof over our heads, Ted; as so many people had been made homeless – due to the bloody war. As you know my dad was a farmworker, working alongside the land girls. Dad's hands were too crippled to serve in the armed forces. He was canny enough to find us a tenanted cottage, where if the monthly rent was paid on time, we kept a roof over our heads.

Grandma worked in domestic service and she told us kids that her contract ended on the 25th of December. Those who lost their jobs had to 'box up' their belongings on the 26th of December and leave the premises – that's why they call it 'Boxing Day', Uncle Ted."

"I know that!" shrieked Ted in frustration at having to listen to his nephew's whining.

"I did not come down with the last bloody shower! Thomas, we both experienced childhood poverty. I had hoped that servitude would disappear once the war was over, especially when our soldiers returned home to Blighty. I had hoped that the working man's unions and fellowships would have shown those bloody toffs, that they could not push us all around anymore. Your old dad used to say,

"'Toffs cannot wash their own backsides', without the help of servants.'

"My old dad also said that it will be a shock to the upper classes, when they have to clean their own houses and dig their own gardens; as most returning soldiers will leave farm work.

"It was a well-known fact that pay is higher in industry. Sometimes, lad, good things evolve over time and those bloody 'Poor Houses' will disappear forever, you can be sure of that!"

Thomas nodded his head in agreement and his Uncle Ted smiled graciously at his nephew's respectful attitude.

"Tell you what, Ted, neither of us knew what it was to have new clothes and after our grandad died, Mum and Grandma cut his Sunday suit down for me, so I could look decent for a better paid job, which would take me out of farming."

"What job was that, Thomas?"

"A coal yard, a few miles from home. It was not a bad pace to work and they taught me to drive their big wagons. I got to earn more money, because my wages increased to fifteen shillings a week, but it did not go far; especially as most of it went on my board and lodgings. I did manage to save enough money to purchase a second-hand motorcycle though, after my first year's employment there.

I stayed at the coal yard until called up to do my National Service. I received a letter, telling me to report to the local Army Recruitment Office.

Once my initial army training was completed, I became a qualified driver but drove mostly Land Rovers and Lorries, but sometimes, I chauffeured officers around."

Ted replied,

"Funny how life has a way of working out without one really trying, Thomas! I always felt that our fate was set out from birth and it was the right thing to just go along with it; that is unless one takes the wrong path – as my old granny used to preach,

'God fearing young men don't take the wrong path.'"

Both men laughed at the thought of their old grandmas' giving them a clip across their ears, just for even thinking such a sinful thing.

"Makes one wonder though, Uncle Ted, how we all managed to fit into those small cottages with just two double bedrooms upstairs, a small sitting room downstairs and a small scullery. I remember the washing boiler in the old scullery, where a small fire was lit underneath it, to heat all the hot water.

Hot baths were limited to once a week, so Saturday night was allocated 'bath night'. Everyone needed to be clean and tidy, ready for church service the next day. There we stood in our undies, lined up, waiting our turn to take a plunge in an old tin bath that was filled with hot water, which had been heated in the washing boiler. The lower down the line one was, the soapier the water became, as that block of Carbolic soap became slimy on the skin."

"Yes," Ted added, "my parents used a similar system, as Saturday night bathing took place in front of a blazing fire. Each child helped to fill the bathtub with water. We took turns to carry jugs of boiling water from the old fire-backed boiler to the old tin bath and blankets were placed over the clothes maid, to allow privacy for each bather.

After bathing, we were given our supper and sent to bed, leaving the sitting room free for the grownups to take their turn in the old tin bath.

Mother laid out our clean clothes on the bed at night, so the family were ready for church service the next morning. Goes without saying, 'Sunday Best' clothes were only worn for church, weddings and funerals; so, we changed into our 'everyday' clothes when we arrived back home."

Thomas explained to his uncle,

"There was a dark passage leading from the scullery to an ant ridden pantry which had only one small window facing north, where the most perishable foods were stored. Mum's seasonal preserves were carefully stacked in line on wooden shelves, that Dad had made from old, wooden planks. I loved Mum's pickled runner beans, red cabbage, onions, and eggs, plus, her tasty fruit preserves and jellies. It was the coldest place as it faced north, so Mum placed her homemade pies in there too and sometimes leftover rabbit stew was left to sit upon the cold floor in heavy, cast iron, black saucepans to be reheated for the next meal."

Such happy memories made them both feel happier, and Ted shared another family memory,

"My family practised good husbandry and prudence too by putting excess seasonal vegetables into hessian sacks and stored them in our old cellars.

Your grandad – my dad – was Head Gardener at the local hall, so he would save several of his best potatoes and slice them crossways, then place them in line on wooden trays. The reason being to allow the potatoes to sprout shoots, which he then planted on for the next season. Such prudence saved our family money.

Our old pantry was so damp that an abundance of mould and mildew grew on the walls, and ants invaded too.

Dad put us children to work each spring, whitewashing the inner walls of the cellar and pantry, using a homemade lime wash, as it helped sanitise them.

The ground floor areas were tiled with red floor tiles laid directly onto the ground, held in place with rough, light mortar, which kept the downstairs cold and made mopping easier for Mum.

Meals were cooked upon the open coal fire situated within the sitting room because it was the warmest place in the house.

There was a wooden pine table, surrounded by various odd chairs in the parlour. Next to the open fire was an old Queen Anne chair, a three-legged side table that was just big enough to hold a teacup, saucer, side plate and ashtray for Dad's pipe. It goes without saying that this chair belonged to the head of the household – my dad!

No one would ever consider disrespecting him by sitting in Dad's chair except his old favourite Greyhound called Gyp.

"We all sat around the table to eat, do our homework, watch Mum sew and mend socks and stockings late into the night, with only a gaslight to work by.

More often than not, we children sat quietly, watching Mum cook our meals, while Dad sat in his chair, reading the newspaper on a Sunday afternoon. Sometimes, Dad read an article he thought was suitable for us older boys to hear on a Sunday evening."

Both men sighed, as the images of that childhood scene flooded their minds. Nostalgia overcame Thomas again, and he said,

"Uncle Ted, do you remember our mums' cooking puddings and cakes in large, cast iron double saucepans?

Water was placed in the bottom half of the pan, to stop the pies burning or cooking too fast."

Thomas licked his lips at the thought of homemade treats as he stated,

"Our family's favourite treats were sugarless puddings, which Mum made from fresh farm butter and honey from the local beekeeper.

As eggs were rationed, she used to barter for an extra portion of egg powder. I can see her now mixing all those ingredients together, adding flour we had collected for her from the local mill. You know, Ted, the mill which adjoins the canal, close to the village!

Sometimes, if a birthday or special occasion were due, she'd mix a cup of Camp Coffee and add it to the mixture. She then poured the pudding mixture into her brown, heavy duty, earthenware bowl, wrapped the whole thing in muslin and tied it into a loose knot at the top. She then slid a sizeable wooden spoon through the knot so the puddings could be lifted easily in and out of the top half of the skillet. We children watched her every move, anticipating the treat that was in store for us all."

Ted smiled at his nephew, his answer was, "Christmas pudding with Brandy Sauce was my favourite. Mum always put a sixpence in her pudding, because on Christmas day, whoever found the coin kept it."

"Brandy Sauce, mate! Bloody hell, you lot lived like kings! Mum poured corn flour sauce, sweetened with honey on our Christmas puddings," retorted Thomas.

Not to be outdone in the memory score, Thomas asked his uncle,

"Do you remember, Ted, how only the big boys completed the heavy chores. Such as chopping up 'morning sticks' for the fire."

"That was because your dad did not trust the girls to use a hand axe safely," smirked his uncle.

Ted continued his reminiscence, "I do remember from my teenage years when occasionally, an old tree fell down, either through age or after being struck by lightning, during winter storms.

The village menfolk worked together to chop it into small logs. Afterwards, the bounty was shared among the relevant families.

Logs were stacked under each family's old, wooden lean to, situated next to the outside lavatories.

The wood sat under cover to season and allow the logs to dry out, ready for our winter fires.

It was in times like those, that poor neighbours helped each other, and it helped to reinforce bonds between many families, which in turn allowed many friendships to blossom.

Tell me lad, was your landlord as mean as ours?"

"Let me put it this way, Ted. The landlord was quick to collect his rent the day Dad got paid but blind to all the repairs that needed doing at our cottage.

Dad knew the rent had to be paid before we all ate, or we'd end up without a roof over our heads and he always got a receipt when he paid our landlord as he just did not trust the miserly old sod.

Like you, we all left school at fourteen, and were expected to contribute towards our room and board. My sisters either worked in service or on the farms. Whereas we boys were encouraged to get an apprenticeship in the building trade, or engineering by our parents.

We were expected to 'better ourselves'. "Well! That is what Dad used to say.

The most Dad or any of us could earn each week was fifteen shillings, and any extra money would have to be received at weekends by doing a 'foreigner', or the taxman took it out of our wage packets. Dad was classed as 'casual labour' which meant he could be 'laid off' from a contract anytime, which meant he got little extra money in his wages. It was an unspoken rule in our house, that we all pooled our money for when one of us needed extra money, Ted."

"What do you mean?" asked his uncle.

"Well! When our kid got his apprenticeship at a local builder's yard, he needed to acquire a basic tool kit and although he applied for a grant from a local charity, it did not cover all his needs. Therefore, we all put our hands in our pockets to make sure he started off on the right foot – so to speak," said Thomas.

"Guess that is what being part of a family is all about," replied his Uncle Ted.

Reality Check

Thomas found great comfort in having shared childhood memories with his Uncle Ted, and told him so,

"Who'd have thought that having been born over a generation apart, we have been given a chance to be united – if only for a short time."

The two young men paused momentarily to take stock of their situation but when they turned to their right, what they saw astonished them. That reality check made them blink their eyes several times to comprehend what stood before them.

Ted proclaimed,

"I said you would not see those old cottages again, Thomas."

Their old childhood cottages were replaced with a newly renovated two storey, red-bricked cottage.

"So 'spick and span' with a brand new Welsh slate roof," Thomas proclaimed in amazement.

Thomas's eyes were fixated upon them.

"Look at that beautiful Silver Caravanette parked upon the cottage's Herringbone, brick driveway, such opulence!"

The soldiers shook their heads in astonishment as Thomas whispered to his friend,

"Where have the old terrace cottages gone? They stood in that very spot for generations, mate? I presumed they would be there forever!"

Thomas's pal looked deeply into his nephew's eyes, put his arm around his shoulder to portray empathy and pleaded to his companion,

"Come on, old pal, let's just accept time has changed everything and as far as I am concerned, good riddance!" He paused for a moment then loudly spouted out,

"Let us not dwell on the past, time is running out and we have not yet reached our destination! Time to leave – come on, put one foot in front of the other. Quick march, soldier!"

The two soldiers proceeded onwards towards the village itself and nervously moved their heads from side to side and observed dramatic changes, which conflicted with their precious memories. With trepidation, they walked forward – still anxious, yet 'in step'; an old habit that soldiers acquire, and the fact that their journey was bound by a quest should have brought comfort to their restless souls.

"Let's sing an old tune together as we continue our journey, what song do you know that is jolly, Thomas?" said Ted

"Err… let me think… How's about 'A hunting we will go'?"

"Can't you think of a more appropriate tune than that!" laughed Ted.

"Alright, let me think – how about that lovely old hymn, 'Onward, Christian Soldiers'?"

Ted nodded his head, looked at him in approval and they burst into song,

"Onward, Christian soldiers,
Marching as to war,
With the Cross of Jesus
Going on before,
Christ, the Royal Master
Leads against the foe;
Forward into battle,
See, His banners go!"

"Stop, stop. Please stop!" cried out Ted in despair.

Thomas asked, "Whatever is wrong, pal? I thought it was good cheery hymn for soldiers."

"I know, lad! It is too perfect – perhaps, it reminded me of our unpredictable quest," refuted Ted.

Vision of Hope

Both men shivered when their bodies cast fearful shadows before them, but Thomas said as a joke, which lightened their mood, "Well! That is a first, we have seen our own shadows at last."

Both men knew that it was no joking matter because they experienced a foreboding, ice-cold chill which ran down their spines and the two unified soldier's relaxed mood came to a sudden halt; as a thunderous storm appeared before them, and blocked their way forward.

The skyline was filled with turbulence. The soldiers could no longer stand upright and were forced to fall down onto their knees. As they fell down, they were imprisoned by a dark evil presence.

Looking into Ted's eyes, Thomas perceived a fearful dread, as his uncle proclaimed,

"Time has caught up with us, my friend, tomorrow is already here! The evils of this cruel world are trying to confine our immortality."

"I do not understand," Thomas cried out in fear.

The swirling winds encircled the two men, and as the circle became tighter and tighter, Ted held onto his nephew with all his strength, and shouted into his right ear,

"While we are together, we are strong, Thomas! Hug me tightly and do not let go, no matter what you see – just focus upon my face. Do not turn your head, no matter what you may hear. The evils of the dark side are trying to separate us, and if they succeed, all is lost! We must remain united to defeat these unholy demons, as much depends upon our unfailing resolve!"

Suddenly, their bodies were ripped and torn to shreds by the demonic forces, only dust remained upon the ground; which was dispersed by the four winds of evil. Nevertheless, the transfiguration of the two men's souls ascended into the heavens of tranquillity.

Having been conveyed into that celestial light, Ted looked deep into his nephew's eyes, hypnotised his nephew, and slowly their two minds became one. Ted's spiritual strength and knowledge had transcended within his nephew, Thomas.

While in that trance, Thomas experienced another vision, which showed him two separate futuristic pathways for mankind. That supernatural apparition showed Thomas two distinct dimensions, which in turn affected both time and space. Both men acknowledged that a Holy War was to take place, and mankind's need for redemption required the intervention of God's Heavenly hosts to defeat the invading satanic demons.

Those Heavenly hosts stood resolute, and after a timeless moment of respite, their merged minds foresaw Earth from the Heavens and it appeared to them through a dense, swirling mass of storms that engulfed the Earth, and they kept watch and contemplated mankind's fate.

Those angels watched Earth's landmass become barely visible, as storms raged, then merged into one giant superstorm.

Ted heard his companion's thoughts,

Is this the same vision which I experienced earlier? For if it is, I fear my resolve is weakening as I sink into despair.

Thomas's angelic companion reassured him when he answered,

"No, Thomas, this is your second vision, where you can help to change man's fate but only if you freely choose to give up your earthly desires, hopes and dreams, and replace them all with an unselfish act of piety."

"How do I show my piousness?" replied Thomas.

His angelic host whispered, "Remember your utmost desire when you arrived home? Your quest was linked to both your love of life and those from your past lifespan, whom you loved!

"Now is the time for a more devotional kind of love! One which will transcend the survival of all life forms on Earth – not just mankind."

Thomas, held tight within that angel's wings, asked, "How may I, a humble soldier, complete such a mission?"

The angel whispered softly, "But, Thomas, you are not just any soldier, but one of God's Christian soldiers!"

"So, I am! My main quest for returning home is clear to me. I am ready! May God guide me and help me to do my best," prayed Thomas.

"Then your transformation is complete, Thomas. Fear not! For thy Lord God, and my Heavenly hosts will guide you."

Thomas's angelic companion whispered gently, "Choose the right path forward and complete a more unselfish act and your true quest will be revealed, Thomas. Help us 'Messaging Angels' to save Earth and guide mankind to a simpler, less selfish, and hopefully more sustainable way of life. Which in turn, will benefit both mankind and all life forms upon Earth itself. What will eventually happen in the future will be for the best, so keep the faith, Thomas."

Thomas's soul was revived when he heard this answer to his prayer and his courage returned as both he and his companion, Ted, found themselves back on Earth.

"Seems that we are to continue our journey," announced Ted.

Thomas opened his eyes to see his companion next to him and found it hard to grasp the reality of their present situation, his uncle.

"My goodness, Ted, did we actually ascend into the Heavens? Or was it a dream?"

"Yes, our ascension saved our souls from the demons, but no! It was not a dream. Our souls are back within our Earthly bodies, for we may encounter people who are sensitive to Heavenly hosts such as you and I." explained Ted.

Renewed Strength

With renewed strength in their bodies and determination in their minds, the two friends marched forward in unison. Their fast walking pace slowed down when before them appeared an apparition of an old bridge.

They both fixed their eyes on that sturdy, ancient, blue bricked bridge situated just a few yards in front of them. The bridge allowed access over the canal into the village of Haven, which was the soldiers' former hometown.

The soldiers seemed relieved to find an old, recognisable landmark and they proceeded towards it with gusto. When they reached their target, they decided to stop momentarily in the middle of the bridge to get their bearings. Both men removed their kit bags from their shoulders and dropped them at their feet then stood at ease.

Ted asked Thomas, "Fancy a smoke, lad?"

Thomas replied instinctively, "Could do with a ciggie, mate. Pass one over here then!"

Ted pulled out his silver, military cigarette case from his left trouser pocket, admired his initials E.B.M. inscribed in gold on the front of his silver case. He then turned slowly towards his nephew and said,

"Here you are, lad, one of my special, hand rolled ciggies. Help yourself."

Thomas pulled out a cigarette from his uncle's silver cigarette case, placed it in his mouth and waited for Ted to offer him a light.

Ted then took out another cigarette for himself, reached once more into his trouser pocket and pulled out his battered, silver plated, military cigarette lighter. That lighter had a symbolic gold crest of a lion on its lower section. Ted flicked open the lighter's top, blew on the wick, flicked the wheel, and it ignited into a bright flame, which allowed him to light both his own and his companion's cigarette.

Thomas noticed the initials on his uncle's lighter and said jokingly,

"I've always found it amusing that once a person was given a nickname, it sticks, and people rarely refer to us by our Christian name."

"So, right, lad. Until I joined the Navy, I had hardly ever been referred to by my Christian name, Edward, and I agree as all my Navy friends called me Ted too!"

The two friends took 'time out' deeply inhaled the cigarette smoke and as it escaped through their nostrils, the smoke circled above their heads. They lifted their heads high and amused themselves when they watched their exhaled smoke form circles above their heads. Ted's smirked expression portrayed pure enjoyment and satisfaction as the tobacco tantalised his taste buds.

Much to the amusement of Ted, Thomas teased him when he said, "Well! Angelic hosts or not, we have not been forced to give up all our Earthly pleasures," he paused then continued his self-mockery,

"I had presumed we'd have to display more virtue, but here we are, enjoying a smoke."

"All Earth Angels' were human once, Thomas, and while we are in contact with mankind, we have to adapt to let our principal character shine through. Otherwise, how would we be able to help people if they cannot relate to us?"

"Never thought of it that way!" answered an amused Thomas.

"Well, now you know!" said Ted with tongue-in-cheek.

The friends burst into spontaneous laughter, then relaxed as they took in the view that was before them.

Ted seemed focused upon the village and muttered,

"What a pretty village we left behind us, mate. Look at all those colourful canal barges moored down on your left, adjacent to the old working mill."

Thomas turned around and observed the scene, while Ted blurted out excitedly,

"Look, Thomas, the Queen's Arms, the pub is still there! Such a shame we have not got time to call in for an ice-cold pint of real ale. I sure fancy a glass of dad's favourite beer, called 'OLD TOM'. What do you say, Thomas?"

Thomas understood the joke and accepted his companion's wishful thinking and answered,

"Life just is not fair sometimes. It would have been nice to down a pint or two, as I can smell the ale from here. The taste of strong, black stout with a full, creamy head on top, would have gone down my throat a treat."

They both laughed and Ted gently slapped his nephew on the back as a gesture of friendship and empathy and said,

"Even angels have a sense of humour! Even after death, life is still what you make of it, lad!"

Thomas looked suspiciously at his uncle, and declared jokingly,

"Stop it, you're splitting my sides open. Stop fooling around mate!"

Ted smiled and suggested, "Let us enjoy another cigarette old chap, and then I'll be ready to move on."

Thomas wagged his finger at his nephew, and in good spirit said,

"Hey! Less of the 'old chap if you don't mind. Remember, I am only three years older than you – even if there was a generation between us – what a cheek!"

Thomas gave out a titter and pulled a funny face at his uncle.

"Now, I know for sure you are taking the piss out of me!" answered Ted.

Ted threw back his head and proceeded to have a fit of the giggles and they both laughed heartedly, so much so that his uncle Ted pleaded,

"Bloody stop it, you're splitting my sides open, have you never heard the saying, 'It only hurts when I laugh', stop it."

After a short while, the young men resumed their composure, long enough to light themselves another cigarette. While they stood still, they focused on the pub's entrance door and Ted said,

"It must be lunchtime as so many customers have entered that front door, but only a small number have left."

Ted cried out,

"I wonder if any of those lucky people ever lifted their pint glasses to honour the 'fallen' – notably today?"

"Why today?" replied Thomas.

"Don't you know what day it is, lad?" asked Ted.

"No idea, Ted," Thomas paused, deep in thought.

Thomas then realised that his companion was serious and asked,

"Is it Remembrance Sunday, Ted?"

His uncle shook his head in disbelief before he replied, "I thought that by now you'd have gathered that fact, but apparently not."

"Well, blow me down, I'd never have guessed – what with it being such a lovely summer day when I arrived home. I thought it was the middle of June, not November 11th."

"We thought you understood, but it seems I have to spell it out for you. Is that right?" answered Ted.

Thomas nodded his head in bewilderment, as his uncle explained,

"It is all about the timeline being distorted, lad. Do you understand?"

Thomas's face was distorted with confusion, his uncle went on to say,

"Death is not the end, my lad, it is just a new beginning! When we die or should I say, pass on to the afterlife; time has no meaning. Sometimes, the timeline opens up into different dimensions. That is what has happened thus far to us!"

Thomas looked confused, so his uncle continued to explain,

"How else did you expect you and I to be able to meet, after all, we were born a generation apart, so we are from different time zones.

"Hence, when you arrived, it was springtime for you, but as our journey progressed, we moved through different dimensions and the timeline adjusted to enable our travels to make sense in our minds.

"One could say that we are time travellers because we have stepped out of man's concept of time."

Thomas's face was quite serious when he declared, "Time has no meaning! Is that what you mean, Uncle Ted?"

Ted outstretched his arms, placed his hands gently upon his nephew's shoulders, and reassured him when he said,

"Time is an undefinable element within the universe, lad. It is a continual progress of existence, as events in the past, present and future are inter-linked.

Therefore, our time together is without limitations, so long as we keep the faith and stay on the path ordained for us."

"Blimey, Ted, you don't half talk highbrow stuff, you ought to have been an officer. I understand – least, I think I do!"

"That will do for now then, lad, but let it be clear in your mind the reason why we are here, together, at this particular place in time.

"It is not our place to judge or question, just obey and stay united until our quests are completed."

"I do understand about the time element, and we have become a good team as 'Seekers'. So, let us do this, and do it well," said Thomas, confidently.

As the time travellers took a long, last look at the canal and pub scene, their morale had fortified, they were more unified and filled with a sense of renewed purpose.

Haven

Thomas and Ted finished their last cigarette and finally turned away from the canal scene and looked towards the village of Haven itself. Both men set their eyes upon a row of newly, renovated terraced cottages squeezed between several shops lined up in a row; which consisted of a Co-op, newsagent, electrical shop, Tearoom and Betting Shop.

Their synchronised stare observed several men, who rushed into the betting shop while they waved betting slips that they held tightly in their hands.

"Looks like someone has enjoyed a win on the horses," said Thomas. The soldiers laughed so much, they almost choked on their cigarettes.

"You look deep in thought, Thomas," said Ted curiously.

"I was just wondering what other surprises fate has in store for us, Ted?" said Thomas.

Bored with the betting shop's activities, the soldiers turned their attention to the left-hand side of the square. Their eyes were drawn towards a newly built fire station situated between an old, large Victorian house and a garage.

"Just look at that red shiny, new fire engine," shouted Thomas with excitement.

"Bloody hell! Have you ever seen anything as beautiful as that, mate?"

The fire engine excited the two young men, so they made haste for a closer view, and when they approached the nearby garage, they observed a line of various cars that waited in line to be served with petrol. A tractor driver started to bellow at the cars in front of him as he had lost his temper,

"Can't you lot bloody hurry up? I have not got all bloody day, you know! I've got a farm to get back to and the work won't get done without me."

In his temper, the red-faced farmer steered his tractor closer and closer to vehicles lined up on the forecourt and blocked the entrance.

"Looks like we'd better move on, I can see a fight breaking out here," said Ted.

Further up to the right, just beyond the fire station, they observed another pub, much to the soldier's delight and Thomas said to his mate,

"Look, mate, the White Lion is still here. I spent many hours knocking back the pints there as a youth and chatting up the local girls. Happy times."

He then took a deep breath and let out a sigh that vibrated through his whole body, which resulted in a momentary judder.

Thomas's Uncle Ted sensed his nephew's despair and he decided that they should dawdle for a while. Indeed, it did seem strange that no one had come to greet them and make conversation with them, and he too felt overpowered by sadness and disappointment engulfed them both.

Haven Village was busy, as it was a market town. Historically it was mentioned in the ancient 'Doomsday Book'. Tourists flocked there in the summer to enjoy its quaint historic buildings. It had a beautiful, ancient Norman Church which sat majestically on the highest spot, and in the of middle the village itself.

Tourists often stayed in the local hostelries which provided Bed and Breakfast facilities, whereas evening meals were provided by the village pubs; which also provided evening entertainment. Residents and tourists alike enjoyed the village pub's evening entertainment, which brought about many lively conversations and sometimes fights broke out on occasions.

Such regular influx of visitors allowed the village's economy to prosper, grow and flourish. Local business kept up with the modern world and many branched out and diversified; which in turn satisfied the ever-demanding needs of the local tourist industry.

The farming community supplied hostelries with fresh produce, and provided a Bed and Breakfast service, which supplemented their incomes and added to the economic growth to the local economy.

Haven was a friendly community where everyone knew their neighbour and people converged in the village square on market days; chatted, gossiped, and took part in village festivities. No stranger entered that village without being noticed!

Therefore, when Thomas walked towards the centre of his old village, he had high expectations of being greeted as the returning hero; especially as the square was inundated with people.

Both soldiers noticed that all the car parks were full, and many cars were parked on the right-hand side of the main road. They stood back and watched people going backwards and forwards into pubs and shops. They could not believe how much the village had changed and grown since their last visit home, and Thomas said,

"Gosh! Look at them all sitting outside the local cafés, drinking, enjoying light meals and chatting away as if they have 'all the time in the world'."

Ted too seemed surprised but stated,

"Last time I experienced a continental style café was in Chile, and I never would have believed this scene if I had not seen it with my own eyes."

As they stood outside that café, they noticed the daily menu board,

"Thursday! It says, 'Thursday's Menu', Ted. No wonder it is so busy. Thursday is market day – if I remember rightly," declared Thomas.

It was indeed Thursday and the Old Buttery situated within the Market Square had several market stalls that sold a variety of goods.

Ted was filled with delight at seeing so many people happily going about their daily business and leaned over to Ted as he said,

"Blimey, the place is filled with locals and tourists alike in the square today. Daresay, they are all looking for bargains."

The soldiers enjoyed the pleasant buzz as they observed old friends who greeted each other. Locals' mingled with visiting tourists' but were astonished to see so many people in one place.

However, it was Thomas who spoke first to his uncle,

"It must be Queen's Day, the busiest day of the week, if I remember correctly."

"What's that supposed to mean?" replied Ted.

"It's the day the old cronies collect their state pensions from the Post Office, of course!

"Thursday mornings after collecting their pensions, the older women busy themselves shopping, but always seemed to find time to gossip," he sniggered, then added, "meanwhile, their husbands enjoyed several pints of ale and a pork pie in the pubs.

"There is nothing more amusing, than standing back and watching people go about their business on a Queen's Day."

The soldiers chuckled then gazed in amazement at how busy that significant day was.

The Encounter

Thomas and his Uncle Ted continued their walk towards the Old Buttery Market, when the soldiers saw a group of girls in front of them. The soldiers smirked then walked forward to where those pretty girls stood.

Thomas slowly, removed his red beret with his right hand, folded it neatly and placed it into his left pocket.

"Come on, let's chat them up, eh, Uncle Ted." For a moment, he had forgotten he was no longer visible, and his mouth jumped in before his brain, when he said,

"It has been such a long time since I was able to 'chat up' a pretty girl, mate! What do you think?"

The two companion soldiers tentatively approached the group of girls. The girls neither flinched nor turned around to acknowledge those two young soldiers. Thomas noticed the girls' attitude of indifference and said to his mate, "Maybe that snub was a pretentious 'come on'," so he winked at each girl in turn, but the girls chatted and giggled amongst themselves.

Thomas was not easily deterred from making a conquest, so he turned, faced his uncle Ted once more and said,

"Not bad, eh, how about that big blonde with the long, slim legs, what cha' say, we give it another try?"

Ted looked his nephew straight in the eye and blurted,

"Idiot! One would think that have you never seen a girl before."

Thomas turned to face his friend, but Ted had already moved away. Thomas's face flushed as he moved awkwardly away from the girls. While Thomas ran to catch up his uncle, he grumbled,

"Ted! You left me standing there like a bloody idiot. Why did you have to be such a goodie-two-shoes."

Ted replied, "Come on, we've got to hurry, keep your mind on the task at hand." Ted left his companion confused and again bellowed at him, "Come on, come on, hurry up!"

Thomas changed his slothful pace and ran, until he had caught up with his impatient uncle.

After he had dropped his head in shame, Thomas said, "Sorry, Ted. I forgot myself for a moment back there."

"Apology accepted," replied his uncle.

Suddenly, the air turned bitterly cold, when a robust wind emerged from the East and replaced the heat from the sun, as a fearful chill filled the air and both pals shivered uncontrollably.

"Have you ever got the feeling that someone just walked over your grave?" whispered Ted.

They were both locked in an aura of dread as silence replaced those delightful sounds of chirping birds.

Their eyes met instinctively, and with teeth tightly clenched, their face muscles locked. They pursed their lips and their senses were overwhelmed with fear. They stood frozen to the spot upon which they stood.

To their right, stood a beautiful ancient oak tree in full leaf and its spread eagled branches watched them. Their eyes glazed over as an unseasonal gust of wind swirled energetically around the tree. The whole tree shook violently, its upper branches hovered lower and lower towards them, blocked out the sunlight, engulfed the two men with its shadows, and day turned into night.

Thomas cried out to his companion, "I have angered him!"

To which, Ted, whispered, "Be silent, Thomas."

Without warning, those oak leaves rustled gently, before flying magically into the air which left the soldiers mesmerised.

When the leaves hit the ground, a thunderbolt struck that ancient oak tree and it burst into flame, then fell onto the ground, barely missed the soldiers which left them petrified! Before those young men had time to react, that dark mass of leaves had blanketed their trembling bodies and with fixated eyes and ashen white faces, Thomas and Ted were imprisoned by nature.

Eventually, nature's grip of death finally released them, and the oak tree's leaves rose up over the soldier's heads and swirled violently around the men.

At that point, both men shouted out in terror, "Please God, forgive us."

The soldiers tentatively watched the leaves hover around them, released their bodies and left them free from restraint; they dropped down on one knee, piously, and prayed together, "Please God, we humbly ask for forgiveness. Amen."

The violent spiralling winds subsided, the leaves fell gently onto the cobbled stone ground – just for a microsecond, then a more gentle, warm breeze gracefully swept that mass of leaves towards a hawthorn hedge opposite them where they settled.

Miraculously, the sun reappeared from behind the dark clouds, the melodious sounds of birds filled the soldier's ears, and they breathed freely.

The young men found themselves standing in front of an old Manor House, and Ted excitedly said,

"Look, Thomas lad, it is our old school."

To which Thomas replied, "Our transpose must be for a purpose, Ted! I am wondering why he wished us to reconnect to our childhood."

Ted's expression was one of relief, but his inner fears surfaced, "I am not sure either but being here is better than the alternative!" Both men stared at each other and nodded.

Manor School

After those two friends had recovered their breath, they decided it was alright to enter the grounds of their old school. The entrance gate was closed tight, so they scampered over the wall – just as they had done as children when late for class.

Ted was the tallest of the two, so he gave Thomas a leg-up over the school wall. The ground within the school boundary was higher, which made it easier for Thomas to jump back onto the wall and there he sat straggle-legged and shouted down at his uncle,

"Come on, mate, just take a running jump at the wall and I will catch your hands and give you a pull-up."

In the excitement of that moment, they almost landed on the other side of the school grounds on top of each other; where the sounds of juvenile laughter filled the air.

Thomas ran ahead of Ted, across the playground, and looked back and saw his uncle, and shouted,

"Let's go find our old classroom and see if our desks with our initials carved inside them are still there."

The playground was full of teenage pupils, but the two pals passed them bye unnoticed. Maybe those schoolchildren were just too engrossed in their own world to notice two uniformed men.

The soldiers stopped directly in front of a Pine double door – which was the main entrance to the building and found it ajar. Casually, they strolled past the girl's cloakroom towards the headmaster's study which was across the Main Hall and down a long, dark passageway, until it ended at the boy's cloakroom.

To their left were large double glass doors which barred their way, and Ted said in his excitement,

"This is it! I am sure that beyond that door is our old classroom. What do you think, Ted?"

Ted answered with the nod of his head, so Thomas cautiously placed his hands around the brass doorknob of that imposing door; turned the handle slowly clockwise and pushed the door open.

Both men tiptoed their way forward and found themselves in a brightly lit room. A room that was filled with row upon row of school desks, which faced a large pine, teacher's desk that was situated in front of a giant blackboard. Several wooden backed dusters sat upon the narrow shelf located below the blackboard.

The two men were transformed into teenagers and in their minds' eye, their uniforms had been replaced by hand-me-down grey short trousers, grey socks up to their knees and brown lace-up leather scuffed shoes. Blue ties formed into loose knots, sat within the middle of their white shirt collars and grey, woollen blazers, heavily worn at the elbows, which completed their uniformed schoolboy look.

Thomas noticed his uncle had an old catapult which hung out of his left trouser pocket and laughed. After they had explored their trouser pockets, they discovered handfuls of various sized glass marbles.

The transported boys sat down on a seat directly behind a double desk, and as Ted placed his catapult on the desk lid he grinned at his nephew.

Thomas asked, "How about you swop me that catapult for six marbles, Ted?"

Ted shook his head and replied, "Not on your Nelly, mate! Make it twelve, and we have a deal."

So, as typical teenage boys, they fidgeted, because Thomas was bored after he had acquired his catapult and wanted to look around for his old desk.

"Quick, quick, come over here and check this desk out," shouted Thomas.

"Have you found them?" asked Ted.

There they stood, utterly gobsmacked! Situated three rows from the back of the room were two identical single desks side by side. They were filled with nostalgia. Both boys lifted up the desktop closest to them and checked the desk's underside for scratches or names.

"Look, my name is on this desk. It is barely visible as so many other names have been scratched into the wood with a penknife, but it is there."

His fingers carefully followed those faint scratched names, then he spelt out,

"Thomas. Yes, I remember using our Johnny's penknife to make my mark during my first day here."

Ted checked out his own desk lid, but could not see his name and looked disappointed, so said,

"My name is not on there, mate!"

His nephew determined not to allow his uncle to be disappointed, declared,

"Perhaps it is somewhere on the top of that desk. Shut the top lid down and recheck."

Ted followed his pal's orders to the letter, scrutinised all the engraved names of generations of pupils who had sat at that desk. Both men were engrossed in the search for Ted's name when suddenly, his uncle spotted a familiar name scratched into the wooden pine desk, close to the inkwell,

"Blimey, Thomas! Here it is," he spelt out his name, Edward.

"Edward!" repeated Thomas.

"Remember I told you Ted is an old accepted nickname for Edward, didn't I," said Ted.

Both men found their discoveries amusing and laughed heartedly.

The two pals wondered around that classroom, lifted up the pine lids of each desk. They examined the engraved names, questioned each other as to whether they remembered any of the names that they had managed to decipher.

The boys within those excited pals ran from classroom to classroom, opened cupboards, writing desks and left chalk marked messages on each of the blackboards, for those new pupils of those who attended their old school to read.

"That'll test our ability to communicate," stated Thomas.

"Are we the only two angels to leave a message behind?" asked Thomas.

"Goodness me, no! There are multiples of angels who belong to the lowest order of angels, spreading the same message throughout the world at this precise moment in time, Thomas. We are the Messengers, and our concern is for the survival of all living things on Earth.

"Our prime aim is to warn mankind of the imminent catastrophe; in the hope that our spiritual message will help humanity to seek redemption."

"What about all those warring countries, will they be able to read it and seek peace on Earth?"

"The seven Archangels are the Guardians of Nations and their concern is with politics, military matters, trade and commerce. Therefore, leaders of nations will be influenced by them – not us!" replied Ted.

"What about those peoples who refuse to repent and follow or live in the shadow of evil. What will happen to them?"

"Followers' of the dark one is not our concern, lad; they shall perish," added Ted.

Thomas stood up, deep in thought for a moment, digested that knowledge, then smiled and said,

"Well! There is always a chance that at least one person may 'shine'.

"That is what my old grandma used to call people who are contacted by the spiritual world, or their senses are attuned to a presence from another dimension."

"Goodness me, I couldn't have put it better myself," answered Thomas.

Both men were enthusiastic to reach out to one living soul and decided to act before time ran out.

Time belonged to no one, and just as they begun to enjoy their childhood experience, Ted was startled by the sound of children's voices and running footsteps which headed towards them.

When those glass doors swung wide open pupils pushed and shoved each other to get to their allocated classrooms.

A loud and authoritarian voice shouted out to the pupils,

"Quiet now! Your break time is over. Stop running, children. Walk into your relevant classrooms in an orderly fashion."

An elderly, heavily built woman, dressed in a black teacher's gown, now stood directly in front of the two friends, and much to their amazement, looked around suspiciously.

They watched her enter the Science classroom next to the boy's cloakroom and were startled to see her stand directly in front of the blackboard and read aloud the message they had written in chalk.

Flummoxed by having read the message out loud to her pupils and without thinking of the consequences, she panicked, turned, hesitated before she said,

"Err! I did not mean to read that message out loud children; so please take no notice of what was written upon the Blackboard.

She then picked up the board duster and wiped away the chalked message. That task deemed harder than she had expected as no matter how hard she tried to obliterate the message; a faint trace of the written words remained upon that board.

The teacher trembled as she tried once more to rub out the angel's message with her board duster, which left her classroom of pupils aghast; especially as the woman whispered under her breath,

"I thought this place was haunted and now I know for sure it is!"

Nevertheless, that teacher was determined to take back her self-control, so she turned around, faced her pupils, and announced,

"This afternoon, we will welcome the Reverend James, who is going to give a lecture on revelations. Please stand up children and welcome our guest speaker for today."

The Science pupils all stood to attention and clapped their hands as they greeted their guest, who walked into the classroom.

A tall, dark-haired, middle-aged man dressed in black church robe and a white starched collar around his neck entered the classroom; and when he did, bumped into the two soldiers. His response was,

"So sorry, young men. I did not see you standing there for a minute. Please accept my apologies."

To which the teacher and her pupils froze, as they watched two blurred images leave their classroom.

When the two pals looked back longingly at the classroom scene, their feeling of nostalgia overwhelmed them to see children happily engrossed in their classwork, without a care into the world and a worried Ted proclaimed, "Time to move on, eh? Seems to me that this visit is meant to remind us both of the importance of our quest, as it may involve saving innocent children's lives," stated Ted.

Thomas reiterated, "Time to move on!"

Thomas's sad frown invited his uncle to remind him, "Places may change over time, but children are so resilient, they reinvigorate a community."

Thomas smiled, for he knew both he and his uncle were kindred spirits and added, "It certainly was a joy to be amongst the living again. The sound of children's laughter reminded us both that they are the future; and as such need to be protected from all the evils of this sad world."

Thomas looked long and hard at his beloved uncle, as he realised the true meaning of Ted's former statement. Tears overflowed from Thomas's eyes, and he pinched his nose and gulped. Thomas felt the need to explain himself,

"Uncle Ted, wait a minute. Listen, I now understand, you see. Despite our strange jumps through time!"

Thomas took a deep breath, then continued, "I arrived back home in such a confused state, my mind being overloaded with memories. Memories that I had held dear while serving in the armed forces. Memories which we soldier use as self-protection, while in dire situations. I did not set out to be selfish or self-obsessed.

"The sudden realisation of finding myself back home confused and frightened the shite out of me. I'd concluded that my quest was linked solely to my family, but as our journey has evolved, I now understand it is far more complicated than that!"

Thomas dropped down on his right knee submissively.

Ted placed his hands upon his pal's shoulders reassured him, when he said,

"Don't' worry about it, lad. Its' alright. What is meant to happen is for a reason! Here, take my hand and stand straight and proud, for you have done nothing to judge yourself so harshly. It is time to move on."

The two pals took one last look at the school's playground and gave out a deep, longing sigh. A sigh that signified tiredness – that can never be explained or defined but it was their way of saying farewell to the innocence of their childhood.

The two soldiers walked side-by-side back up that lonely hill called, School Lane. They stopped and paused when they reached the top.

The sun reappeared again from behind a dark cloud, lit up the old Norman Church that stood high upon its mound. As they lifted up their eyes, they saw an angel of the Highest Order situated on top the church's steeple. They felt blessed, knew their quest was not fortuitous and the apparition of that Heavenly host meant their first quest was forthcoming.

The soldiers continued their walk and found themselves situated on the other side of Haven. They were sad that no one was around to experience that wondrous event. Nevertheless, those two pals were filled with joy when they crossed the main street and walked up a small dirt track lane.

"We both seem to have experienced a form of time travel, which allowed us to participate in the present, while seeing visions of two separate and totally unpredictable futures for mankind. This journey is just the beginning of a greater spiritual journey for you and I." Announced Ted.

"May I presume that when we leave Haven, we will be going our separate ways to fulfil our individual destiny?" asked, Thomas.

"You presume right!" answered his uncle.

Decision Time

The old dirt track opened out at the top, into a crescent of twenty newly built, red brick houses. Each set of dwellings' front gardens led to a front door. There was also a side path that led to their backdoor which gave the residents access to their coal house and washhouse, linked by a flat roofed corridor.

The soldiers stood and stared at that new scene, for neither of them had ever been there before.

Ted broke the silence when he said,

"Well! Looks to me as if we have moved forward in time and the question is, Thomas, how far into the future have we moved?"

Thomas stood mesmerised when his eyes were drawn towards a specific house and in his excitement cried out,

"Look to your right, Ted, No. 19 is Mum and Dad's new house for sure. Look! A little girl is playing with her friends outside on the lawn. She is the spitting image of my youngest sister, Pinky, with those long blonde plaits tied at the bottom with yellow ribbons. Yes! Its' Pinky! Lets' move closer, Ted."

When those two onlookers moved forward, they seemed to be held back by a swirling vortex, which spun around the two soldiers so fast, that they both blacked out!

When the two pals finally opened their eyes, the scene before them had changed. Children were no longer on the front lawn of No. 19 but replaced by an ambulance which was parked immediately in front of Thomas's mother's house, and its siren loudly blared out. That loud noise awakened the curiosity of the other residents within that street, and curious neighbours gathered around the ambulance vehicle, keen to find out what had happened to their neighbour.

Thomas watched an elderly man who had approached the driver of the ambulance and asked him,

"Who is sick?" He then shouted out to the crowd, "It's her mother! She has suffered a major heart attack. It does not look as if she'll make it."

Ted turned to face his companion. Thomas's face portrayed trepidation. Ted placed his arms around his nephew and consoled him, but his pal cried out,

"We're too late, and it is all my fault. I am a dawdler and it has cost Mum her life. Oh! How selfish I am. May God forgive me." He sobbed openly upon Ted's shoulder and was inconsolable.

Shortly afterwards, the crowd of onlookers gathered around and watched two ambulance men who had appeared out of the front door of No. 19.

The two medics shouted at the group of people,

"Please move away from the ambulance and house. We need room to carry out this lady and place her safely in our vehicle."

The onlookers complied, formed a walkway and the two ambulance men carried the woman out of the house, wrapped in blankets on a stretcher.

A neighbour rushed forward, opened the backdoors of the vehicle and the medical team lifted the woman from the stretcher, onto a couch inside the ambulance.

A District Nurse who followed the ambulance to the scene, also left the house, ran down the path and climbed the steps of that ambulance and sat down next to the sick woman.

The ambulance driver closed the backdoors of the van tightly. He then walked around to the front of the ambulance, eased himself onto his seat, started the vehicle's engine and it swiftly moved away from that crescent of houses.

Relatives and neighbours looked on anxiously.

"Where are they taking her?" an old neighbour asked one of the woman's sons.

"To the hospital!" the son replied.

"We'll follow the ambulance in my old car. Go, get what you need for her now and I will go and return home for my car keys."

"Are you sure you do not mind?" asked the son.

"It is the least I can do for a good neighbour and friend. There is no time to go catch a bus. If we hurry, we can arrive at the hospital shortly after the ambulance. Does your dad want to come along too?"

"No, he is at work! I have sent my brother to the farm where he works, as to tell him what has happened."

Thomas and Ted had decided to walk back down the lane, but when they reached the bottom of the lane, they noticed that the ambulance was parked at the bottom of the lane and its backdoors were wide open.

The two distressed pals ran over to look inside to see a nurse giving the woman artificial respiration, whilst she said to the driver,

"Stop here! Do not drive off yet. Her heart has stopped again. Pass me the oxygen kit from that cupboard under the seat. I may need to inject her with adrenalin." The medic followed the nurse's orders to a T.

A grief stricken Thomas stood frozen to the spot when suddenly, he heard a softly spoken voice that came from somewhere behind the two pals.

Thomas and Ted instinctively turned around and were astounded to see Thomas's mother who smiled sweetly at them both, before she said,

"Hello, son, Ted. Now this a surprise for an old woman. Two handsome young men waiting for me. Have you come to take me to heaven, son?" she cried out anxiously.

Ted, said to the woman, "Well, hello to you too, Maisie. You are still as pretty as when I first saw you on your wedding day. I always said you were a class above us all, and here you are!"

The old woman turned, looked at the nurse who was still working hard to save her life and said,

"She is wasting her time – angel, that she is! I have no regrets. I have had a long and full life. Now, I just want to be rid of all my pain and enter that celestial plane. Let us leave, son. Ted, showed me the way to Heaven, He knows I am tired."

She turned back and looked directly at her son, Thomas, as she said,

"The day – no, moment you died, I went blind and instinctively knew you had been shot.

"Indeed! I felt the bullets enter my chest, just as painfully as you. I apparently collapsed. I do not remember anything else until I awoke up in hospital two weeks later.

"The doctors told me that I had suffered a severe heart attack. Although I returned home two weeks later, I was not myself and suffered a nervous breakdown.

"I ended up at a convalescent home in Wales. I grew strong there, learnt to drive a car in those two years. They helped me get well and strong-minded again, and I did not want to return home, but start a new life, free from poverty and its burdens."

Thomas and his uncle listened attentively to Maisie's pleas, but she knew by the way they looked at her, her confession had shocked them to the core.

Maisie continued to explain in a truthful manner,

"It is so easy to judge, son, but you both knew how difficult life was for me – especially my experiencing three heart attacks before the age of twenty-two years. Having one child after another, despite my weak heart, only made my heart condition get worse.

"I had no respite until I was past child bearing age. Your dad was no help, being an active, family orientated man, but he eventually accepted how things were meant to be between us. He tried his best and was never out of work, and if it were not for his gift of being a good gardener, we never would have survived."

Thomas looked at his mother's tear stained face, placed his arms around her and gently hugged her.

Despite seeing the deep pain in her eyes, he whispered gently into her right ear, "I understand, Mum. I love you more than life itself. I appreciate the sacrifices and compromises that you made for us but what about our little Pinky? Surely, she cannot survive without a mum to love and guide her as she grows up!"

Thomas's mother cried uncontrollably, and her son understood her plea for eternal peace. He wrapped his arms around her and comforted her.

Nevertheless, Thomas's mother's plea was an unexpected complication and he felt undecided how to fulfil his quest, as ordained by a higher power that neither of them could have imagine.

Thomas looked at his uncle to assess his reaction and in doing so, noticed silent tears that streamed down his face and dropped silently onto his jacket. Thomas's stern expression and attitude were felt by his mother and she released herself from her son's embrace.

Ted suddenly stepped forward and said, "Explain your dilemma, lad! Your mother understood that I am sure of. Go on, explain your visions."

Thomas took hold of his mother's cold hands, squeezed them gently, kissed each finger with the gentleness of an angel. He smiled affectionately at her, then declared,

"Mum, I believe I am meant to fulfil several quests before I can receive my beloved wings!"

His mother's eyes were transfixed upon her son's eyes but tried her best to understand what was entirely incomprehensible to her. She wanted so much to understand, help her beloved son achieve his quest, as suddenly she felt her son's pain which helped her understood his dilemma.

Thomas knew his duty towards his mother conflicted with his ordained s quest. Yet, his personal quest was to be there, when his mother died and help her pass over into Heaven itself. He wanted to fulfil her last wishes but something deep inside his very soul told him that his duty to God came first.

He blurted out, "This is not the right time, Mum! You are not supposed to give up so easily on life. Life is precious and complicated. It was you who told me to, 'Come back home safe,' and you taught me to 'fight for our existence, if need be!'"

He smiled gently, squeezed his mother's cold hands and told her, "Your daughter needs you and God has a purpose for her. She will not live a long or healthy life, but she will make a difference to the future of mankind if you return to guide her along her critical path to enlightenment."

"You are determined to send me back then, son! Is it indeed your belief that I can do what you ask of me?" asked Thomas's mother.

"I truly believe that your influence will help her to realise her full potential and fulfil her destiny, Mum."

"Well, what you have said is very profound! Who'd have thought that an ordinary soldier such as yourself could play such an essential part in the survival of mankind."

Thomas laughed out loud and hugged both his uncle and mother, before he replied,

"Guess I am no 'ordinary soldier' – nor is Ted, just your brother-in-law! We are now Christian soldiers, angels of the lowest order whose task is to help save those believers who follow the right path and forsake the dark side of life. This is the time of angels, Mum! Mankind's ruin and annihilation will follow; if we do not compete our quest. The Apocalypse is nigh, and time is running out fast! Will you consider going back?"

Ted stood beside his sister-in-law, took hold of her right hand, and said,

"Maisie, it is your choice! You can choose to take hold of my hand right now and God will think no worse of you. You will enter through the Gates of Heaven – just as you hoped for. Take a moment! For this decision is not Thomas's to make! No, indeed, it is solely your decision, Maisie. God will love you, whatever you decide to do, for you have already gained your place in Heaven."

Thomas looked on. He had not expected that intervention by his uncle and it seemed to him that he was so wrong to think that he could demand his mother's return to life. Initially, Thomas had been convinced that when he asked his mother to sacrifice her own needs over her daughter's, it was the right thing to do; but now he understood that it was wrong.

"Ted is right, Mum, only you can make this decision. We love you and whatever you decide, we will be here for you!" declared Thomas submissively.

Thomas understood his mother's heartfelt need to be appreciated as a human being in her own right – not as a mother, daughter, friend, sister in law or neighbour. She just wanted to be accepted as a person in her own right.

Maisie turned away from her brother-in-law, pulled her hands slowly out of his gentle embrace.

Her focus was upon on the ambulance, the nurse determined to bring back life to that lifeless body which she had once inhabited.

The thought of going back into that lifeless shell petrified her. She called out painfully,

"Oh God, give me the strength to do what is right. I cannot decide so quickly, it is just too much to ask of a weary old woman. Amen."

The two soldiers watched as Maisie was surrounded by an intense bright light and her body glowed brightly. There was a gentle, simple but contented smile upon her face and her arms were outstretched in a relaxed and accepting manner.

Both men assumed she had indeed made her decision and they bowed their heads before they knelt down on one knee to pray and to show their respect for her.

Before the pals dared lift up their heads, they felt a gentle, submissive tap on their shoulders.

With caution they lifted their heads looked upwards towards the heavens but were astounded to see that Maisie stood in front of them wearing a broad, friendly grin on her face.

"Surprised you both then, eh? You thought I was a goner then? Go on admit it!" she explained her celestial experience,

"I have never, not ever, experienced such peace in my mind before. My very soul was touched by a healing spirit, and I knew that although I'd decided to leave, it was not too late to change my mind. I had only one request to make to that angel,

"'Please, I do not wish to remember this incident, for it would play on my mind, and stop me from enjoying the life I have before me.'

"I was assured that when my time arrives, I will enter gently into that celestial light for all eternity. I told them I did not wish to be an angel like you, and they granted that wish!

"So here I am, ready to say my last 'goodbye' to you both. I shall no longer grieve for you, my son. I shall live on for my remaining family and enjoy each God-given day I have left here on this fateful Earth."

Thomas and Ted gently embraced Maisie. For yes, she should be addressed as 'Maisie'; for she had become a person in her own right at last, and decisions concerning both her and her family were hers to make.

"Goodbye, sweet mother, and thank you," cried out Thomas.

"Goodbye, Maisie. My brother was truly blessed when he fell in love and married you. Thank you. Don't forget to have some fun along the way!" concurred Ted.

Suddenly, Maisie looked young again, after the removal of all that human sorrow and grief which had burdened her for too many years. She stepped lightly up the steps into that ambulance and gently became at one with her physical body.

Meanwhile, the ambulance driver ran around from the front of his vehicle to help his colleague, as a relieved and delighted nurse stated,

"The pulse is getting slowly stronger. We can move off now and proceed to the hospital. I think this one is a born survivor. Thank the Lord."

"Amen to that!" replied the ambulance driver.

The soldiers stayed around long enough to watch Maisie's neighbour catch up with the ambulance before the two vehicles sped off towards the nearest local hospital.

"Well, that is one of your quests successfully completed, Thomas. You learnt the real importance of allowing each person to make their own decisions, without interfering or influencing them. That, my lad, is the accurate indication of a real angel."

Both men embraced, and laughed joyfully until Thomas turned to face Ted and asked him,

"What do you mean 'one of my quests'? On second thoughts Ted, please, do not answer that question."

They knew that their future was already set out before them and that acceptance had released them both of physical pain and mental torment, which was replaced by serenity and contentment.

Thomas and his uncle happily marched on in step as good soldiers did. They crossed a minor road which led them away from Maisie's home.

There was a narrow footpath before them, on the right-hand side of a narrow gradient, which was the shortest access route to the village church upon which they continued their questful journey.

Period of Darkness

Before those soldiers reached the top of the hill, they were stopped suddenly in their tracks when the skyline appeared to be on fire; after a massive blast occurred.

Thomas cried out, "Bloody hell! Look, a missile has just passed overhead, and it seems to be heading Eastwards."

"Where?" asked Ted.

"Look up, it's high on the Eastern horizon," replied his nephew.

The ground around them turned deep red, as uncontrollable winds circled the village and the soldiers heard screams of anguish from afar.

Intense winds almost knocked them off their feet when the force of the explosion hit them.

It was at that precise moment they observed a woman run down the hill towards them. She was holding onto her black umbrella and gripped the handle of her brolly, as if her life depended upon it – despite the fact that those savage winds had already blown the umbrella inside out!

When the woman reached the two soldiers, they saw terror in her eyes as she pushed past them! Before the woman disappeared out of view, she let out a piercing scream and the brolly fell from her hand.

The two speechless soldiers found themselves frozen to the spot, until the heat blast from another explosion knocked them off their feet but they gained their composure almost immediately…

They proceeded up that small hill with caution, braced their bent bodies against the oncoming force of that treacherous wind, walked in single file and Thomas led the way.

When they finally reached the top of the hill, Thomas turned around and asked his friend,

"Are you alright, Ted?"

Ted nodded his head.

By the time Thomas faced forward, visibility was zero and a dense fog engulfed them both and a breathless Thomas declared,

"It is a little early in the year for freezing fog."

Both men shivered from head to toe and Thomas shouted, "Are you still there, Uncle Ted? I cannot see you. In fact, I cannot see anything."

"Yes. Reach out for my hand. I am directly behind you," replied Ted.

Thomas did what was asked of him, which enabled his pal to stand by his side. Ted embraced his nephew's invisible body as he said, "I've got you, lad, fear not!"

His reassured companion whispered in his uncle's ear, "This fog tastes foul. Reminded me of past winters when smog was so poisonous, people wore muslin facemasks to protect them from breathing in airborne toxins. It was never as bad as this! It is enough to make one throw up and my eyes are burning too."

"Keep your mouth shut then, Thomas," replied Ted.

Although Ted's comment amused them both, laugher would have exposed their throats even more to that vile stench. So, they stood still and close together, closed their eyes, then waited, and waited!

Fate Catches up

When the soldiers finally opened their eyes, the fog had disappeared and the two men found themselves sitting upright on the top step of the entrance to the village church, covered from head to toe in a blanket of snow.

Ted asked his drowsy friend, "I wonder how long we have been sitting here, Thomas? My mind is groggy and confused. I feel as if I have been forcibly woken up from a deep, traumatic sleep or should I say, nightmare!"

Thomas had awoken before his uncle, which gave him time to observe his surroundings in more detail. With troubled eyes, Thomas told his uncle, "Blimey mate, when I awoke, Haven Village was covered feet deep in snow. Look for yourself, not one living soul to be seen for miles. The whole village looked to me as if it had been deserted for quite some time."

"Did you dream, Thomas, while in that trance-like state?" questioned Ted.

Thomas stood up, shook the layer of snow from his uniform, shivered uncontrollably. He then placed his right hand on a snow-covered iron railing situated next to his right-hand side. His torso was numb down to his toes. He looked down at his friend and said,

"My mind is muddled. I'm not sure, but I seem to remember fragments of a dream."

He hesitated, shook his head, placed his open palms around his head in despair and because his legs were weak and wobbly, he sat back down on top of the snow next to his friend.

"Well! What do you remember then?" insisted Ted.

"It's very fuzzy," he replied.

Thomas took in a deep breath and as the ice-cold air entered his lungs he gasped, then continued to explain,

"I'm not sure yet whether it was a dream, or it actually happened. Tell you this, mate, this situation looks terrifyingly like the after effect of a nuclear winter!"

Ted asked questionably, "Surely not! You experienced two visions remember, and one was the lesser of the two evils, remember? I pray the latter one would save mankind – not destroy it."

Thomas moved closer to his Uncle Ted. He sought the comfort of another being and it seemed to him that he needed to explain his dream in more detail.

"In my dream I found myself adrift, floating high in the atmosphere where I was able to watch a dreadful superstorm develop.

"This time, the whole scenario felt different from my second vision. I do recall the first storm was caused by man's abuse of nature.

"This storm was different though, for it seemed to start after I perceived hundreds of rockets being launched from within Earth's orbit itself. I heard multiple unified voices from afar, saying,

"'All MIRV missiles must be launched at the exact same time. We are now in God's hands.'

"What puzzled me was that they were launched from silo bases all over the world, and they were aimed outside Earth, towards space itself.

"This fact focused my mind and I turned away from Earth to focus my eyes outward towards space. I sensed a presence of evil long before my eyes saw it! I felt dense darkness enter my mind, almost paralysing my very soul as a vast, dark shadow approached Earth at an unnervingly controlled high speed. It was too large to be anything linked to our planet and it was at that point I realised mankind was at war with an alien life-form.

"While my mind was linked within that darkness, I saw enormous, grotesque demonic creatures in vessels like no man had ever seen before.

"They were aware of my presence and were trying to read my mind, but I fought hard and long against them. I finally built up a brick wall in my mind to block the demons out and prayed continually.

"Eventually, my mind was my own again. I knew for sure that those demons had telepathic abilities and as such, were able to link into other and enter in to more vulnerable or willing humans on Earth.

"Believe me, Ted, all I could do was use the power of prayer as a weapon against them. God only knows how those wretched victims of their mindset suffered down on Earth, for it was painful – even for me.

"Remember my first vision was linked to an alien's 'Scorched Earth' effect, Uncle Ted?"

Ted nodded his head in acknowledgement. Thomas continued,

"That dream was different, because mankind was united in fighting an invading force of Evil, instead of nation against nation.

"I believe, we humans won the war, but the after effect was that several superstorms changed Earth's climate; to such an extent that a mini nuclear winter evolved. I do believe that is why we found ourselves here in the depths of winter; where our surroundings seem devoid of all human life.

"Nevertheless, I sense life forms from all over our planet Earth and that gave me hope that mankind had survived, but I am not sure how.

"I do not have the answers! I am no scientist, but I am sure that we need to travel forward in time to find out exactly what has happened. For someone knows exactly what happened and what will happen next."

Ted interrupted his nephew, "We need to know if our army of angelic hosts completed their missions. If they did triumph, they would have saved those who were deemed necessary for mankind to become more compassionate and less selfish; thus, allowed both the survival of humanity and Earth. Let us pray for a moment, for I am sure we are in the right place but apparently, not in the correct time zone."

"Yes, I agree. We need answers, but my gut instinct tells me to go forward in time, not backwards.

"I am sure that once we understand what happened we will be able to complete our final quest and move on," reiterated Thomas.

"My goodness, Thomas, you really have earned your wings, pal."

11-11-2039

Without thinking but using their instincts as a guide, both soldiers rose from those cold steps, shook off the snow, turned around and faced the enormous oak studded doors of Haven's church.

Although snow had drifted as high up to the church door's heavy iron handles, they both placed their hands upon that icy door latch and turned simultaneously, pushed with all their strength against the door to open it.

The old door creaked and groaned and eventually moved slowly inwards – which allowed the soldiers to pass through a small gap, into a small porch area. They quickly turned around, closed the double oak doors which stopped more drifting snow enter the church's porch.

The church porch was a sparse cold and empty room and looked more like an ice palace from a fairy tale book than an entrance room to a church.

"The ancient stone seats on each side of the porch are still here," said Thomas.

"Yes! But with snow cushions," laughed his Uncle Ted.

Directly in front of them was a closed single oak door, studded with nails in the form of a cross. A large iron ring was attached to that ancient lock and Ted immediately walked towards that door, lifted the massive, icy ring in both hands and turned its lock clockwise.

The old door groaned and groaned loudly, and Thomas sensed a fearful dread.

"My goodness me, I felt a chill run down my spine when that door creaked; it sounded like a cry from the grave!" cried out Thomas.

"Shh! Listen up, lad. I can hear muffled sounds coming from the other side of this door. Can you hear it? Sounds like human voices," replied Ted.

Thomas stood directly behind his uncle, helped him to push that ghostly door ajar. The groaning was so loud, it reminded Ted of a ship-wrecked vessel, being battered by rocks below the surface of the sea. Such a thought sent a severe judder through his cold body.

To their great delight and surprise, they realised that a melodious sound of song greeted them as the door slowly opened, and yet, they were not able to see a single soul, as they peered through that small gap. Cautiously they continued to walk up several stone steps, that lead to the church's inner sanctum.

When they reached the top level, they found themselves amidst a small congregation of people singing praises as a white bearded old man sat on an old leather seat, doubled over the keyboard of an ancient church organ. The man's crippled old fingers were barely visible beneath finger gloves and he hit the organ's ivory keys determinedly, whilst he tried his best, with a croaky voice, to lead his congregation into song.

Thomas and Ted's eyes strayed away from the organist towards an old wooden notice board, and the details that had been carefully written upon it in chalk.

The first soldier to speak was Ted,

"Look, Thomas, at the date on that hymn board, it confirms that we have moved forward in time," he spelt out the written date: "11.11.2039."

Both men were transfixed momentarily until Thomas declared,

"We seem to be visiting Haven Village once again on 'Armistice Day', that must be a significant fact in itself, Ted."

As the parishioners sang out the hymn, 'Abide with me', the two pals sat down on a rickety, old and dusty pew at the back of the church; situated next to the old studded double oak doors known as 'The West Door'.

The scene set before them was like nothing they had ever experienced before, and they sat silently and allowed their senses to comprehend that strange congregation.

The soldiers estimated there were at least 200 adults of various ages who sat tightly together, thus filled row upon row of pine pews. That congregation were clothed in layer upon layer of smelly old materials that were ragged. Most of the parishioners were draped in dirty, old blankets of various colours and materials over their attire, to keep out the intense cold, which even Thomas and Ted experienced.

In between the pews were various forms of bedding spread across the floors, down each aisle and in every crack and crevice. There appeared to be many children – once again of various ages, who ran freely around the church like wild gaunt, half-starved beasts; yet happily played 'tag' and their screams of excitement almost eliminated the sound of the organ.

"It seems these poor souls have been here for quite some time, Uncle. Look! Those rags strewn on the floors seem to be where they sleep and eat."

It was hard for the soldiers to guess the age of many of the people, as men wore heavy beards and women wore muffled scarves around their faces and heads as did the children.

Suddenly, Thomas spoke softly to his companion,

"My God! They look like refugees – not parishioners. The scent of human waste and sweat in here is enough to knock a donkey off its feet – as my old mum used to say, Ted."

"Have you noticed the icicles hanging from the ceilings and iced-up windows? They have tried to blank-out the freezing winds with old carpets. I expect they tried their best to keep out the freezing cold, but I wonder if it was also their way of keeping their sanctuary safe from any marauding outsiders. I never thought that I would see open fires like these in our church.

"It, beggars' belief, that anyone survived such conditions for so long – considering how perishing cold it is outside. The old concept of a church being the perfect sanctuary in the Dark Ages seems to have been reinstated here! Anyway, it is the ideal haven for these pitiful survivors, Thomas."

"It is God's House!" cried out Thomas, and he placed his hands together and prayed for these poor souls who seemed so close to death.

Thomas was stunned by the fortitude those few survivors had shown, and he was mesmerised by their sincere piety when he listened to their croaky voices hit the high notes as they sang their favourite hymns.

He whispered his own prayer, "Please, God in Heaven, have pity on these poor wretches, for they portray their faith most humbly and such people are mankind's hope for a better future. Amen."

The congregation stopped singing! The organist led them in a prayer for deliverance. As the soldiers watched those forlorn lost sheep fall to their knees in prayer, they too joined the congregation's prayers and silent tears flowed down their cheeks.

"Oh! Almighty God. Please look down upon your lost sheep with pity on this sad day. We are truly, sorry for our past sins and trespasses and ask for your forgiveness.

"Notably, in our minds at present is the welfare of our innocent children, who deserve a better world; where compassion and selfishness overpowers the dark side of life. Amen."

Before anyone dared to rise, the organist said a final prayer,

"Almighty God in Heaven, you delivered us from the evil demons that tried to conquer our beloved planet, Earth, and we are truly thankful. Amen."

The united congregation responded,

"We are truly thankful. Amen."

The organist walked to an old wooden pulpit which overlooked his congregation. He placed his right hand upon a large leather-bound Bible and shortly afterwards was joined by three others, whom he had beckoned with his left hand to approach his pulpit:

The first person lifted out a well-worn copy of the 'Tanakh' from his shoulder bag, lifted it high into the air and declared,

"We are all God's children. May there be no more wars amongst men. May there be peace on Earth and may we appreciate and nurture nature and all of God's creatures."

To which the community cried out, "Amen."

A second person stepped forward, and with a copy of the 'Quran' held high above his head he said,

"May we all be guided, united and wise. May we all be enriched by our differences. May we all celebrate now and forever our gratefulness for our deliverance from the evil demons. Demons who once lived amongst us, corrupted us and almost destroyed us all."

The listening and tearful congregation answered, "Amen."

The last person stood on the bottom step of the pulpit, looked around fearfully as the two others stood either side of him, and to his surprise, placed their arms around their neighbour.

He was genuinely fearful and trembled when he declared to those listeners,

"I have no right to be here, standing with these three pious men for I am an atheist. I have never understood the point of believing in anything but my own welfare. Yet, I stand before you now a deemed sinner, who finally understands the true meaning of hope! When the war upon our world began, I followed no religion, no political, cultural belief; except the need to survive, and I did survive."

The silence within this church became deafening as this 'loner' smiled and confirmed,

"Yes! You have the right to judge me, throw me out into the wilderness, or even kill me. For I am a sinner of the highest degree and for that, I am ashamed! Nevertheless, when those demons showed themselves to me as they did to all sinners here on Earth; I denied them! I remember that I dropped down on my knees and prayed to God for forgiveness.

"As the demons tried to engulf my very soul, I cried out in despair, 'God in Heaven, have pity on a poor sinner, who is sorry for not taking both You and our Lord Jesus into my heart. You know everything there is to know about me – I am sure of this. Please forgive me, and I shall follow you – wherever that leads me. Amen.'"

The congregation suddenly ran towards the self-declared atheist, and as he saw them approach him, he stood his ground, whispered to his two fellow companions,

"Whatever happens, now is surely God's will. Stand aside, my friends!"

Thomas and Ted also ran forward, opened their shiny silver wings, and embraced the self-defined sinner.

That angelic vision was witnessed by the congregation and when they reached the redeemed sinner, they joined hands and encircled the atheist and the two angels.

Each member of that community then shook their neighbour's hand, proclaimed their non-judgemental friendship just as the organist announced,

"You are welcome in God's house forever; for now, we are all blessed, and you have brought 'hope' back into our hearts. Thank you."

Suddenly, the massive oak-studded doors shook violently, and the congregation trembled with fear and many dropped to their knees. One by one, they turned around to face their fate! The West Door of that Ancient Norman Church groaned painfully, just as they heard an almighty thud, from the outside. Then, slowly but surely, the old door began to open; grinding across the old wood-block floor of the Church. Snow, had piled up against the outside of the old door, but the congregation realised that someone was trying to get inside; as many mingled voices drifted in through the ever wider gap, which separated them from a lifeless, deathly grave.

"Prepare to defend yourselves," shouted out the Priest.

His congregation were ill equipped to form any kind of defence and hid behind the old Oak Pews.

Panic ensued within the sanctuary of that old Church, and the soldiers watched in horror.

"Ted was the first to speak, "it is alright Thomas, God has intervened. No harm shall come to these poor survivors; he knows that they have suffered enough."

When that West Door opened, the air dropped below zero, everyone's breath froze, and a dense cloud of snow blew into the Church; covering the back pews. It had been months, maybe years, since most of that congregation had felt the sun's rays upon them; they shouted out,

"Hallelujah."

Many of those who watched from within that candle-lit sanctuary tried to protect their eyes from the intensity of those lights and many others fainted in shock. Some cried out in fear, but the bravest ran towards that light, despite the freezing cold air which chilled them all to the bone and greeted the newcomers; who entered their sanctuary.

Those strangers who entered the ancient church, were dressed in Arctic white, survival gear, carried food and medical supplies and one member of that team shouted,

"Hello! Do not be afraid of us. We have come here today to rescue you all. Who is your leader?"

All the onlookers pointed towards the organist who was still standing in the pulpit, looking down upon the rescuers. As quickly as tears fell from the organist's eyes, they froze immediately around his eyelashes; due to the freezing winds that had entered the old church.

Once the doors were closed again, the rescuers went about their business of handing out warm clothing, food, and bottled water; as several medics methodically began to care for the sick, wounded, and starving. A member of that medical team shouted,

"Please, form an orderly line. Women and children will be cared for first."

Everyone complied and once the rescuers were deemed able to be moved, the rescuers called for an emergency airlift via their field radio,

"We have numerous survivors here in Haven. Please send backup resources as soon as possible."

Thomas and Ted watched the soldiers tenderly, aid those people, when they took their first step outside, into that white wonderland. Within the hour, the survivor's faced glowed, from the warmth of the sun's rays.

The survivors were told to, '

"Stand with your backs to the West wall; it will support you and protect you from the cold. Help is on its' way. Have patience and stay close together for warmth."

And there they all stood in silence with their backs against that snowy West wall, full of hope; whilst their stomachs rumbled noisily.

A large man, who seemed to be the Leader of the Rescue squad said to the raggedly clothed survivors,

"You need to wrap yourselves in the Survival blankets, being handed out to each of you. We have sent for air transportation. Enjoy, the food parcels already given to each of you, and enjoy the warm soup from the flasks; which our medics will bring to you shortly."

While the congregation waited for help to arrive, they lit fires with the help of their rescuers and encircled the flames to warm their hands and sang hymns.

Suddenly, one survivor asked one obliging soldier, "What day is it, young man?

To which the soldier laughed before he replied,

"Why, it is Armistice Day, old fella! People all over the world are being liberated and celebrating this special day at this precise moment. For when the bad weather suddenly subsided, it allowed Search and Rescue Teams to venture outside worldwide!"

The old man turned back towards his fellow companions. and said,

"Armistice Day! I cannot believe it!" He then turned around and shouted back at his rescuer,

"Have we missed it?"

"Missed what?" answered the medic.

"The eleventh hour, daft lad! What do you think I meant?"

"God, no! It is only ten o'clock in the morning."

The survivors congregated together, much to the curiosity of the rescuers and the organist shouted out to one and all,

"Let us do it! Come on, everyone, let us too celebrate our liberation from the demons. We shall give thanks to God and show our sincere respect to our fallen comrades, who cannot be with us today."

Several minutes later, six large rescue spaceships landed simultaneously upon the grounds of that old ancient Norman Church. Within minutes, the officers had arranged an impromptu service of thanks.

The organist led his community in prayer,
"Our Father which art in Heaven… Amen."
Soldiers and congregation alike sang,

"Oh God, Our help in ages past
Our Hope for years to come
Our shelter from the stormy blast
And our redeemer home…"

Thomas and Ted watched on as the officer-in-charge took over the community's ceremony and completed the final order of respect towards the fallen.

The congregation congregated around the snowy ancient cenotaph and joined hands as they all chanted,
"They shall not grow old, as we grow old.
Age shall not weary them, nor the years condemn.
At the going down of the sun and in the morning
We shall remember them."

The angelic angels bowed their heads as they heard the congregation speak out,
"Lest we forget."

While the congregation bowed their heads to show their respect to the fallen, Thomas whispered, "It is time for our departure, Uncle Ted. That particular quest is now completed."

To which the commanding officer replied,
"You may think that is so, lads! Believe me, there is much physical and spiritual work to do, as our task to restore our Planet Earth, to its rightful order. The hard work has only just begun. We will meet again very soon, that I can assure you both."

Ted and Thomas looked into the officer's eyes, surprised at his outburst, and asked,
"So, the war to end all wars is not over then, sir?"

To which the officer replied, "Did you not understand, lads, angelic hosts such as yourselves now walk amongst mankind. Without those 'messages' left by both you and your fellow Christian soldiers, we would never have been forewarned of those approaching demon colonists."

"What about the messages from The Seven Archangels, sir?" asked Ted.

"Now, that is where the actual heavenly intervention took place, so to speak! Apparently, seven of the World's Nations Leaders experienced a vision at precisely the same time. The vision showed them the exact place on Earth where a scouting demon spaceship had crash landed many decades ago.

"A United Nation's force discovered the alien ship and our scientists were able to adapt their advanced technology to our space programme. As for the alien pilots, one died due to the impact of the crash and the other was – shall we say, 'useful' as a learning tool; which enabled us humans to learn the alien demon's weakness.

"Ever since the demonic war ended, God's heavenly Angels' have visibly walked amongst mankind. The Angels became our spiritual guides, and now a unified part of humanity's culture," explained the officer-in-charge.

"Well! That certainly explains a great deal, sir… Except, why we two angels, are about to depart into another time, and space." Said Thomas.

The officer bowed low and said, "Goodbye for now, my friends. Till we meet again – very soon. Thank you!"

Everyone that was congregated around Haven's cenotaph, turned towards the two angelic hosts, when a bright light appeared behind the angels; their silver wings sparkled in the sunlight and almost dazzled their onlookers.

A vortex appeared on the horizon where a portal connected those two different dimensions; Ted turned to Thomas, pointed it out, then whispered to him,

"Take another look at that officer, Thomas, have you noticed how closely he resembles your sister?"

Thomas stared at the officer so long that he was asked by that observant officer;

"What is troubling you?"

Thomas hesitated then asked politely,

"Sir! May I ask your name and where you originated from; with those deep blue eyes, platinum blond hair and fair skin?"

The officer and the congregation seemed amused at such a question being asked by one of their Heavenly hosts.

Nevertheless, the young officer answered,

"My name is General Williams. Okay! 'Pinky' is my Christian name, and although it may seem amusing or somewhat effeminate to some, it is an old family nickname! For generations, the name 'Pinky' has been passed down to the eldest son. I believe a brother of one of my Grandmothers', way back in the 20c; gave her the nickname, 'Pinky' nickname, just before he embarked to Egypt. It was shortly before he died during the Suez Crisis. She passed it on to her firstborn boy in his honour, and that is how the family tradition began! May I ask why my name is of such importance to you, young man?"

Thomas smiled warmly at the general, held out his right hand and replied, "Shake hands with your long-lost Uncle Thomas. "The surprise on that officer's face amused Thomas, and he said," I too believe we may indeed meet again quite soon."

Both angelic hosts smiled, for now, they knew that such happenings were quite a familiar occurrence to those enlightened humans.

As the vortex fully opened up behind the angels, it was no longer frightening or strange, but just another Heavenly Gateway for those two Guardian Angels to travel through time, space, and spiritual dimensions.

The two soldiers had fulfilled their Quests, but took but a moment, to view their old Haven village; which had been buried under a mountain of snow and ice, and Ted said,

"Who would of thought that our insignificant little home, would end up looking like a Winter wonderland – totally unrecognisable – if it were not for our old Norman Church, which has stood the test of time."

Thomas smiled, then grabbed his uncle's right hand and said,

"We now go our separate ways Ted. May God, be our guide."

That blinding stream of lights which crowned those two Questful Seekers, blinded people's view momentarily, and shortly afterwards; the Heavens were filled with a joyful sound, of Angels singing.

Epilogue
11-11-3019

"As the rockets soared into the Heavens'-humankind held its breath; for Mother Nature whispered, 'So, You, think you are in charge.' And God smiled.'"

A new world order evolved on Planet Earth, where both angelic angels and enlightened humans lived and worked together as one.

Mother Nature was respected and nurtured, and the World Government, brought forth legal practices; of non-polluting, less invasive forms of transport, communications' and agriculture. Thus, enabling Planet Earth's resources to become more sustainable.

All nations accepted that all of God's creatures are indeed 'Sentient Beings' and as such were legally protected. Man's companion, animals, were accepted as equals and respected; thus, harmony and selfless compassion was finally achieved for all life forms on Earth.

Mankind had the technology to go forth and seek out other life forms in faraway galaxies; which they did but with the aim of Peace.

Nevertheless, the Seven Angels and the Guardian Angels watched over mankind; intervened as and when they deemed necessary.

Mankind had discovered the balance of dimensions and time; which was not allowed to be destroyed; as such mankind was encouraged to stay on the 'Path of Enlightenment', and away from the 'dark side' of life.

"This not the end, just the Beginning!"